BODYGUARD

Book 6: Survival

Also by Chris Bradford

The Bodyguard series
Book 1: Recruit
Book 2: Hostage
Book 3: Hijack
Book 4: Ransom
Book 5: Ambush
Book 6: Survival

BODYGUARD

Book 6: Survival

Chris Bradford

Philomel Books

PHILOMEL BOOKS
an imprint of Penguin Random House LLC
375 Hudson Street, New York, NY 10014

Library of Congress Cataloging-in-Publication Data is available upon request.
Printed in the United States of America.
ISBN 9781524737078
10 9 8 7 6 5 4 3 2 1

American edition edited by Brian Geffen.
American edition design by Jennifer Chung.
Text set in 11-point Palatino Nova.

To Matt, Nicky and Oliver,
survival of the fittest!

"The best bodyguard is the one nobody notices."

With the rise of teen stars, the intense media focus on celebrity families and a new wave of millionaires and billionaires, adults are no longer the only target for hostage-taking, blackmail and assassination— kids are too.

That's why they need specialized protection ...

GUARDIAN

Guardian is a secret close-protection organization that differs from all other security outfits by training and supplying only young bodyguards.

Known as guardians, these highly skilled kids are more effective than the typical adult bodyguard, who can easily draw unwanted attention. Operating invisibly as a child's constant companion, a guardian provides the greatest possible protection for any high-profile or vulnerable young target.

In a life-threatening situation, a **guardian** is the final ring of defense.

PREVIOUSLY ON BODYGUARD . . .

Tasked with protecting Amber, a French diplomat's daughter, and her brother, Henri, on safari, Guardian recruit Connor Reeves hopes for an easy mission but . . .

"Don't drop your guard, Connor," said Colonel Black. Reaching into his desk drawer, he pulled out a battered pocket manual. "Here, something for you to read on the plane."

He tossed it to Connor. The green-and-orange cover sported the title *SAS Survival Handbook*.

"Expecting problems?" asked Connor, glancing up at the colonel.

Colonel Black shook his head. "No, but it's always best to be prepared for the worst. Especially in Africa."

——

The colonel's advice proves all too true when a diamond field is discovered in the safari park and the president of Burundi fears trouble . . .

"The last thing we need is a false diamond rush."

"Should I delay the French diplomat's visit?" asked Minister Feruzi.

President Bagaza repeatedly clicked the top of his ballpoint pen, considering the proposal for a moment. "No. Not after the millions France has invested in the conservation program." He gave everyone at the table a meaningful look. "In the meantime, this news isn't to go any farther than this room. Understood?"

His ministers nodded obediently. But President Bagaza knew it was a futile request. Diamonds lured corrupt men like wasps to a jam jar.

———

Amid rumors of diamonds, a shady deal between a feared rebel leader and a sinister organization is struck deep in the heart of the jungle . . .

"Have you secured the area where the diamonds are located?"

"Not yet," admitted the general. "But with your guns we will."

Mr. Gray pocketed the stone. "Equilibrium will supply the weapons you need on the condition that once you've seized power, they're granted sole mining rights. Agreed?"

"Agreed," said General Pascal, offering his meaty slab of a hand.

Unaware of the impending danger, Connor, Amber and Henri are enjoying their safari when the rebel army moves in . . .

"What's Buju spotted now?" whispered Amber.

"I'm not sure," replied Gunner, switching off the engine. Clambering out of the driver's seat, he went over and began studying the ground with the tracker.

For some reason Connor's sixth sense began twitching.

"What did you see?" asked Henri excitedly.

All of a sudden a lone impala bolted from behind a clump of tall grass. At the same time, a short sharp *crack* punctured the silence. Pivoting in his seat, Connor spotted the president's driver slumped over his wheel. For a moment Connor thought he was just resting, but then he noticed the splatter of fresh blood on the Land Rover's windshield. A second later the president's 4×4 rattled as if being pelted by hail.

"GET DOWN!" yelled Connor.

———

Caught in an ambush, Connor requires all his skills to escape . . .

Gunmen rushed out to surround the Land Rover. But Connor refused to surrender without a fight. With the engine revved to the max, he threw the gearshift into reverse and sped away from the trench. It was a desperate decision to head back into the kill zone. But it was his only option.

The gunmen opened fire, and bullets thudded into the retreating Land Rover.

"You're going the wrong way!" yelled Amber, her face pale, blood trickling from the cut to her cheek.

"Just taking a little detour," he explained. "Hold on, you two!"

———

But the rebel leader wants no survivors . . .

"How could you *lose* three children in a Land Rover?" demanded General Pascal, his tone exasperated.

"They disappeared into the jungle."

The smile evaporated from the general's face. "My orders were explicit. No one must be allowed to escape. No one can raise the alarm."

The general turned to Blaze. *"Hunt them down!"*

1

"I think we've lost them," said Connor, slowing their pace through the bushes.

"I think *we're* lost," replied Amber with an uncertain glance at the encroaching jungle.

Scanning the disorienting tangle of thick vegetation, Connor was forced to agree. His only objective had been to escape the gunmen, so he'd paid little attention to the direction they'd run in. A potentially critical error of judgment. He *should* have been thinking like a bodyguard, assessing the situation at every point and noting their escape route. Now they were completely lost in unfamiliar and dangerous territory, with no backup.

Henri stumbled over a branch and Connor caught his arm to keep him from falling. Wheezing heavily from their mad dash through the jungle, the boy's face was pale and sweaty, and his lips had a worrying blue tinge.

"Where's your inhaler?" asked Amber as Connor guided

her brother over to a fallen tree and helped him sit down.

"*Poc . . . ket,*" he rasped.

Amber fished it out for him. Henri grabbed it as if he was drowning, immediately taking two puffs. A minute went by and he was still clawing for breath. Panic welling in his eyes, he inhaled another two doses.

"Calm down, Henri. Slow, steady breaths," soothed Amber, gently stroking his arm. "We're safe now. You can relax."

Gradually Henri's wheezing eased and his lips regained their color. Closing his eyes, he leaned forward, his head in his hands.

"Will he be all right?" asked Connor, aware that a severe asthma attack could be fatal.

Amber nodded. "He just needs some time to recover." Her gaze fell to Connor's chest, and her pale green eyes widened in alarm. "You're bleeding!"

Connor glanced down. The patch of blood on his T-shirt had blossomed. Gingerly lifting the fabric, he peeled the sodden cloth away from his skin. A bullet had clipped his side, leaving a long gash. His T-shirt, although stab-proof, offered no protection from a 7.62 mm high-velocity bullet, and blood seeped steadily from the wound. As soon as he examined the injury, his brain registered the damage and pain rushed in.

Grimacing, Connor put down his go-bag and extracted the first-aid kit.

"Let me do that," said Amber, taking the kit from him and insisting that he sit down.

Tired and hurting, Connor did as she instructed. Using an antiseptic wipe, Amber cleaned away the blood.

"Ouch, that stings!" he said, wincing.

"Don't be a baby," she chastised, inspecting the wound. "It's not as bad as it looks. I think the bullet only grazed you."

She took out a gauze pad, placed it over the gash and applied pressure. "Hold that there."

Connor kept the pad in place as she found some dressing tape and a bandage. "How come you know what to do?" he asked.

"I'm a junior rock-climbing instructor. First aid is part of the training." She wrapped the tape around his midriff several times, securing the gauze pad and stemming the bleeding. "That should do it."

Connor found a spare shirt in his go-bag and put it on. Amber then turned her attention to the cut above his left eye.

"So, what do you think happened back there? Why were they trying to kill us?"

"They were trying to kill President Bagaza," replied Connor. "We just happened to be in the way."

"Who'd do such a thing? He seems like such a nice man."

Connor shrugged. "Any number of rebel groups in Burundi. My operational brief listed at least four active militia units who oppose him. But I'm guessing it's the ANL–the Armée Nationale de la Liberté—led by a man known as Black Mamba."

"Who?" said Amber, discarding a bloodstained wipe and covering his cut with a Band-Aid.

"You really don't want to know. But he's notorious for using child soldiers. And some of the attackers today were kids our age."

Amber's mouth fell open in shock. *"Kids?"*

Connor gave a grim nod. "My turn to fix you," he said, finding another antiseptic wipe from the first-aid kit.

"I can't believe kids were shooting at us with machine guns! Do you think—" Her lower lip began to tremble and her eyes flicked briefly to Henri before she managed to whisper, "Do you think they killed our parents?"

"Hold still," said Connor, gently dabbing at the cut on her quivering lip.

As Amber sought a response from him, her eyes welled up and a tear rolled down her cheek, washing a thin line through the blood and dirt smearing her skin. Connor wiped it away with his thumb. In truth, he thought it was highly unlikely that Laurent or Cerise had survived the ambush. Their Land Rover had been a total wreck, and if by some miracle they'd escaped the crash unhurt, then the gunmen would have shot them down, just like they had the ranger. But Connor also realized that if Amber and Henri were to survive this ordeal, they needed to hold on to the hope that their parents were still alive.

"I didn't see their bodies. So there's a good chance they escaped like us."

"Really?" said Amber, brightening. Connor could tell she was desperate to believe him.

"The crucial thing now is for us to get to the lodge and contact Guardian."

"But won't this Black Mamba or his soldiers head to the lodge too?" said Henri, who'd been listening the whole time, his breathing having finally returned to normal.

"That's a risk we'll have to take. The lodge is the only property for a hundred miles and, since I've lost my phone, has the only means of communication . . . unless either of you has a cell phone?" he added hopefully.

Henri shook his head. "Not allowed one."

"Sorry," said Amber with a regretful smile. "Left mine in the bedroom."

"Then we have no other option."

Connor packed away the first-aid kit and shouldered his go-bag.

"But how do we even know which direction to go in?" asked Amber, waving her hand around the shadowy jungle.

Connor pivoted on the spot, trying to get his bearings. There were no obvious paths or visible landmarks, and the sun was obscured by the canopy above. And they couldn't retrace their steps for fear of encountering the gunmen. He glanced at his watch. Sunset was less than an hour off. It would be dark soon, and then they'd have absolutely no chance of finding their way back to the lodge.

Conscious that both Amber and Henri were waiting for him to make a decision, *relying* on him to take command, he was about to make a wild guess when he looked again at the G-Shock Rangeman watch that Charley and Amir had given him for his birthday. It barely had a scratch on it. Amir was right; the watch was indestructible. He silently thanked them for their inspired gift as he rotated the bezel and switched to compass mode.

"From what I remember, the viewpoint lay northeast of the lodge, and we've traveled more or less west," he explained to Amber and Henri. "So, all being well, we just follow the compass south and we'll find the lodge."

2

"Are you sure we're going the right way?" asked Amber, panting from the exertion of their trek.

The jungle had thickened, and progress had become painfully slow as they tramped through dense undergrowth and clambered over rotting tree trunks. Mosquitoes buzzed in their ears, a constant irritation despite having doused themselves with insect repellent. In the treetops, monkeys chattered unseen and leaped from branch to branch, sending leaves falling like rain onto the earth below.

Connor wiped the perspiration from his brow and checked his compass again. It was proving impossible to keep to a straight bearing, because trees, ferns and vines choked the jungle floor, forcing them to constantly alter course.

"We need to head to higher ground," he said. "Work out where we are."

Coming across an animal trail, he led them upslope. The

light was fading fast, and the jungle was being swallowed by shadows. Soon they wouldn't be able to see one another, let alone their pursuers. Henri, his eyes darting toward any strange sound or movement, was becoming more and more scared, and he didn't protest when his sister took his hand. The terrain beneath their feet grew rockier as they ascended toward a small ridge, the trees thinning as they climbed. Suddenly, as if they were emerging from a deep dive, the canopy parted to reveal an indigo-blue sky, the first stars of night blinking in the heavens.

Standing atop the rocky ridge, Connor was able to look out across part of the Ruvubu Valley. Using his binoculars, he tried to spot any familiar landmarks. The sun, a ball of fiery orange, was burning low on the horizon, giving him true west. To the south, the Ruvubu River wound lazily through the valley basin. And off to the east, he could make out the craggy peak of Dead Man's Hill. The dried-out riverbed where the ambush had taken place was hidden from view by the trees, but Connor was able to figure out the lodge's rough direction from a single dark line that cut across the savannah. With so few roads, the main dirt track stood out like a scar on the landscape.

"We're a little off course," he admitted, directing their gaze to a midpoint in the distance. "That's where the lodge is. Somewhere on the other side of that ridge."

Amber squinted into the twilight. "How far, do you think?"

"At this pace, half a day's walk, I guess, maybe more."

Amber glanced at her brother, who was wheezing again from the climb. "We need to rest," she said.

Connor looked at both Henri and Amber. They were all tired, hungry, hot and thirsty. They'd been running on adrenaline and shock for the past hour. Now that that was beginning to fade, their bodies were crashing. He nodded in agreement. Finding a patch of clear ground, they sat down and Connor retrieved the water bottle from his go-bag. Barely a couple of gulps remained. He offered the bottle to Amber, who let her brother drink first. Then, after taking a sip herself, she handed it back.

Despite his own thirst, Connor waved the bottle away. "You have it."

"No," insisted Amber, forcing it into his hand. "No heroics. You need it as much as we do."

Connor drank the last dregs, the warm water wetting his mouth but doing little more. Only now did it hit him that they were in a survival situation.

Running from the gunmen was just the start of their problems. The main threat to their lives came from being in the wilds of Africa without food, water or weapons.

Colonel Black's parting words rang in his ears: *It's always best to be prepared for the worst, especially in Africa.* In light of their current situation, Connor thought that the colonel had never said truer words, and he wished now he'd spent more time studying the SAS survival handbook he'd been given.

Recalling that the right equipment could make the difference between life and death, Connor emptied his go-bag and took stock of their resources. He'd lost the most crucial item—his smartphone—back at the crash site, but he did have a small first-aid kit, empty water bottle, binoculars, malaria tablets, sunblock, insect repellent, a flashlight, a single energy bar, sunglasses with night-vision capability and, still attached to his belt, his father's knife.

"What's that?" asked Henri, pointing to a blue tube in the bottom of the bag.

Connor fished it out and smiled, glad of Bugsy's foresight. "A LifeStraw," he explained. "We just need to find water and we can all drink safely."

With one key survival factor half solved, Connor asked, "What do you have in your pockets?"

Amber produced cherry-flavored lip balm, a packet of tissues and a hair band. Henri had a couple of pieces of candy and his inhaler. Hiding his disappointment at such meager offerings, Connor opened the energy bar and divided it between the three of them. "Not much of a dinner, I'm afraid, but it's better than nothing."

The granola bar was gone in one bite, only serving to remind them of how hungry they actually were.

"Is this edible?" Connor asked, half joking, as he picked up the lip balm.

"Tastes nice and keeps your lips soft," replied Amber, "but not an ideal dessert."

Henri offered his two sweets to Connor and his sister.

"Save them," said Connor, smiling at his generosity. "We'll be needing them for breakfast."

Dusk was falling fast. Even with his night-vision sunglasses and a small flashlight, Connor knew that it would be foolish to navigate the jungle at night.

"We need to find a safe place to sleep," he said, repacking everything into his go-bag.

"We're not going back to the lodge?" Henri asked with an anxious glance at the gloomy jungle surrounding them.

Connor shook his head. "Too dangerous. It's best we hole up somewhere until daw—"

A rustle in the bushes alerted Connor to something approaching. He put a finger to his lips, urging Amber and Henri to remain silent.

The rustling drew closer. To Connor's ears, it sounded like more than one person, all converging on the ridge. The gunmen had caught up with them fast! But no doubt they had trackers with them.

Looking for a place to hide, he hustled Amber and Henri into a crevice in the rocks. They lay flat, waiting for the gunmen's approach. Reaching for his belt, Connor unsheathed his father's knife. Although it was no match for an assault rifle, he gained strength and courage from having it in his grasp.

The noise grew louder. Connor could hear Amber's panicked breathing in his ear and feel Henri's body trembling at his side. His grip on the knife tightened as a bush only a few feet away began to shake. Then a snout with two large curved tusks appeared, followed by a large flattened head and a gray bristled body. Snorting, a warthog trotted over the ridge, followed by a litter of young piglets.

Connor relaxed his grip on the knife and slowly let out the breath he'd been holding. The warthog suddenly turned her head in their direction. Sniffing the air, she grunted furiously, flattened her mane of bristles and bolted away, her piglets squealing in terror as they too ran for cover.

Amber laughed, more in relief than anything. "I'm glad there's something in this jungle more scared than we are!" she said.

But as they crawled out of the crevice, they discovered what the warthog and her piglets had really been running from.

3

A harsh hissing sound greeted them, and Connor's blood turned to ice in his veins. Slithering over the rock toward them was a long, slender olive-brown snake. Ten feet in length and with a body as thick as a man's wrist, it was the largest snake Connor had ever seen. As it reared up and challenged them with its dark, malevolent eyes, Connor's chest suddenly tightened and he began to fight for breath. The sight of the snake turned his skin clammy and his fingers went numb, until he could barely grip his knife any more.

"I think we're in its lair," whispered Amber.

The pounding of his heart was so loud in his ears that Connor heard her as if she were in another world. Her voice, distant and ghostlike, drifted through his fearful state. *"We need to move."*

Hypnotized by the creature swaying before him, his limbs had turned heavy as lead. However much he willed himself, he was rooted to the spot by sheer terror.

Amber eased herself away. Henri went to do the same, but as soon as he moved, the snake hissed sharply in warning. Rising three feet off the ground, it opened its jaws to reveal a pair of razor-sharp fangs and a jet-black mouth.

Henri froze. "A black mamba!" he gasped.

Connor now recognized the coffin-shaped head that Gunner had described. *Believe me, you do not want to meet one of those in the bush.*

Face-to-face with his darkest nightmare, Connor couldn't have agreed more. He knew from the ranger that the black mamba possessed the most potent snake venom in the world. Unpredictable and highly aggressive, in an attack it would strike multiple times, injecting lethal amounts of poison with every bite. Within minutes, the victim would experience dizziness, sweating, crippling headaches and severe abdominal pain. Their heartbeat would become erratic, leading to violent convulsions and collapse. The whole body would go into shock, inducing vomiting, fever and paralysis of the limbs. Finally, the victim would succumb to respiratory failure or else a heart attack.

A horrific and agonizing death, whichever way it ended.

All this knowledge only served to immobilize Connor further.

The black mamba, its tongue flicking and tasting the air, expanded its narrow hood and hissed aggressively. It made a mock charge and Henri jerked back in panic. The sudden move triggered the black mamba to strike for real.

Time seemed to slow as Connor battled his phobia, struggling to overcome his self-induced paralysis and protect Henri. But all he could do was watch as the snake's venomous fangs closed in on the boy.

Then a stick came crashing down on the head of the snake, clubbing it senseless. The stick struck again and again until it snapped with the force of the blows, leaving the coffin-shaped head pulverized on the rock.

Amber stood over the dead and battered snake, her body trembling, her eyes fierce.

"I don't know about you two, but I've had enough ambushes for one day."

Connor knelt beside the tepee of sticks, his knife and a flint stone in hand. Feeling as if he was back camping with his father, he struck the edge of the blade against the flint, trying to create a spark and set the small pile of wood shavings alight. He'd had reservations about making a fire. There was a risk that the gunmen would spot the flames in the darkness. But he weighed this against the danger from wild animals and the need for warmth during the chilly night ahead.

They'd found the ideal place to set up camp, a shallow cave a little farther down from the ridge, where a stream ran through a gully into a pool before flowing on through the jungle. Connor had made certain that the cave was empty first, throwing in a stone, then checking the entrance for any signs that an animal might be using it as a den. With no obvious remains of food or droppings, the cave appeared uninhabited.

Connor struck the flint harder. Still getting no spark, he

persisted, becoming increasingly frustrated and worried he might damage the steel blade. His memory of lighting fires with his father seemed to be a simple matter of a quick strike followed by the whole pyramid of sticks bursting into glorious flame. But so far all he'd managed to do was graze his knuckles and blunt his knife.

After ten minutes of futile striking, he was on the verge of giving up when a single flicker like a tiny falling star dropped onto the tinder. Connor blew softly, desperately trying to coax the spark into a flame. But the small glow died away rapidly. Tired and hungry, he tossed aside the flint in a fit of frustration.

"Would this be easier?" asked Henri.

Glancing over, Connor saw he was holding up a small book of matches.

"Where did you get *those*?" he cried.

Henri offered a sheepish grin. "My back pocket."

"Why on earth didn't you give them to me earlier?" Connor said, shaking his head in disbelief as he grabbed the book from him.

Henri shrugged an apology. "I forgot I'd taken them from the lodge's bar. Besides, you looked like you knew what you were doing."

"I don't have a clue what I'm doing!" shouted Connor.

Henri wore a wounded look. "But you're our bodyguard..."

Connor took a deep breath, trying to rein in his annoyance.

"Sorry, I didn't mean to snap at you. That snake freaked me out, that's all."

He struck one of the matches and the tinder immediately caught alight. With a few gentle puffs, he coaxed the flames, and the tepee of sticks began to crackle and burn. "So much for my SAS survival skills," he sighed, pocketing the matches and hoping his father wasn't looking down on him, shaking his head in despair.

At that moment Amber returned with another armful of sticks for the fire. Or at least Connor thought they were sticks at first. Instead she dumped the dead black mamba at his feet. Connor flinched and scrambled away.

"Dinner," Amber explained.

"You've got to be kidding!" said Connor, eyeing the mamba warily, expecting it to come back to life and strike at any moment.

"Remember what Gunner said: snake is steak in the bush. And we need to eat."

Connor felt the ache in his stomach and knew she was right. No wonder he was so short-tempered. Swallowing back his revulsion, he forced himself to crouch beside the black mamba. He reached out a hand to hold the snake's pulverized head in position, but shuddered at the thought of touching the creature's oily scales.

"Sorry, I simply can't do it," he admitted, passing Amber his knife.

"If it was a spider, I wouldn't be able to either," she replied.

Taking great care not to go anywhere near the fangs, Amber used the blade to cut the snake's head off. Then, once the fire had settled down, she laid the body on the hot embers. The skin sizzled loudly, and soon afterward, the cave filled with the aroma of cooking flesh. Despite his phobia of snakes, Connor's mouth began to water in anticipation.

Having each drunk from the pool using the LifeStraw, they sat around the fire and waited for their snake dinner to be ready. Night had truly fallen, and their shadows played out against the cave wall. Insects whirred and chirped, bats fluttered overhead and unseen creatures leaped from the branches, screeching and hollering. The incessant noise of the jungle was unnerving, and the three of them huddled closer to the fire. Somewhere in the darkness they heard a series of low threatening growls, like the sawing of wood.

Amber gazed nervously into the pitch-black. "What do you think that is?" she whispered.

"Whatever it is," Connor replied, "it's a long way from us." Or so he hoped.

After half an hour, Amber tested the snake with his knife. "I think it's cooked."

Pulling the body off the coals, she sliced it open and cut a portion of steaming meat for each of them.

Henri examined his unusual meal with trepidation. "Do you think it's safe to eat?"

"The poison's in the head, according to Gunner, so it should be," replied Amber, sniffing her piece cautiously.

Hunger overcoming his aversion to snake, Connor took a bite. "Tastes like chicken!" he said in surprise.

The other two tucked in, devouring their meal quickly. Once their bellies were full, exhaustion soon overtook them.

"I'll build up the fire," said Connor as Amber settled her brother at the back of the cave.

As he piled on some larger logs, Connor could hear the two of them whispering, their voices echoing off the rock wall.

"Ow! The ground's all stony."

Amber swept away the debris with her hand. "You can rest your head on these leaves," she said, gathering up some green branches.

Henri lay down. "No animals will get us, will they?"

Amber shook her head. "The fire will scare them off. Now go to sleep."

She appeared to hesitate, then leaned forward and kissed him on the forehead. Henri stared up at her, evidently surprised by her unexpected tenderness. Then he said, "Mama and Papa are dead, aren't they?" His tone was matter-of-fact and all the more heartrending for it.

Amber stroked his tousles of red hair gently from his face. "They might have escaped, like us."

"But how could they? They don't have a bodyguard like Connor to protect them."

Amber glanced over her shoulder at Connor. Their eyes met, and he tried to offer her a reassuring smile. She turned back to her brother. "I'm sure they'll be waiting at the lodge for us," she said. "Now close your eyes and get some rest. We have a long day ahead."

Connor could tell from the tremor in her voice that Amber was just barely holding it together, trying not to show weakness in front of her brother. Connor admired her for that. Prodding a stick into the fire, he watched the sparks spiral up into the night. He too needed to appear strong for their benefit, but he felt the weight of responsibility on his shoulders and a knot of deep anxiety gripping his stomach at the fear of failure. If it hadn't been for Amber's brave actions, Henri would be dead or dying by now, poisoned by the black mamba. And it would have been *his* fault. Even now the very thought of that snake sent a shiver down his spine. His phobia had rendered him powerless to protect either of them. He'd not been much of a bodyguard. More a liability. What if he froze again and failed to react? Maybe not against a snake, but a lion or a leopard or some other deadly animal. The incident had sown the seeds of doubt, and he seriously questioned if he was up to the task ahead.

Amber appeared quietly at his side, her eyes glistening with tears.

"Are you okay?" he asked.

She nodded and pulled her knees into her chest. They

lapsed into silence, listening to the snap and crackle of the fire while staring into the flames.

After a while, she asked, "Do you honestly think anyone else escaped?"

Connor thought back to the chaos of the ambush. "Gunner and Buju, perhaps. Also, I'm certain Minister Feruzi and Minister Rawasa and the others in their vehicle did. They're probably raising the alarm as we speak, bringing in reinforcements. With any luck, Buju will be following our tracks and we'll be picked up by a government patrol tomorrow."

Amber rested her head on his shoulder, whether through tiredness or for comfort he couldn't tell. "Thank you, Connor," she said.

"For what?"

"For saving our lives."

Connor went back to prodding the fire. "I'm the one who should be thanking *you*. I was useless against that snake."

"Snake combat isn't part of bodyguard training, then?"

"No, of course not," he replied, before realizing she was teasing him.

"Don't beat yourself up about it. We all have our fears to face. And you've eaten yours!" she said with an impish grin.

Connor laughed. "I suppose that's what you call true revenge."

Amber sat up. "Can I ask you a question?"

Connor nodded. "Sure."

"How did the gunmen know where to ambush us?"

Connor turned to face her. "That's something that's been bothering me too," he admitted. "The attack had to be carefully planned; they'd even dug a trench. So they must have known the route in advance."

Amber's eyes widened in comprehension. "You mean someone told them. But who?"

"Your guess is as good as mine. One of the soldiers? Perhaps a park ranger?"

"Or even one of the ministers," suggested Amber darkly.

5

No Mercy had seen the white boy look straight at him just before the general gave the command to open fire. That second or so of advance warning had undoubtedly saved the boy from a bullet to the head. And despite the number of rounds he'd drilled into the Land Rover, the boy's lightning-fast reactions had also saved the other two passengers from being killed. Much as he hated to, No Mercy had to admire the boy's warrior spirit.

The fact that there'd been three white kids traveling with the president's convoy in the first place had surprised No Mercy. But their unexpected presence ultimately made no difference to ANL's mission objective: to ambush and kill the president and his entourage. It was just irritating that the kids had gotten away.

But they wouldn't be free for much longer.

"Which way did they go?" Blaze demanded of the tracker.

Buju studied the ground surrounding the crashed Land

Rover. His eyes read the confusion of footprints in the dirt, identifying three different sets before his attention was caught by a line of broken fern stems. He pointed west.

"Then let's go," said Blaze impatiently. "They've got a night's head start on us."

With Buju and Blaze leading the way, No Mercy followed with Dredd and two other soldiers from the jeep. The jungle was barely awake, dawn filtering through the canopy in shafts of spectral light, and birds only just beginning to sing their morning chorus. As the unit of ANL soldiers trekked through the undergrowth, the tracker paused every so often to look for another sign—a footprint, a damaged piece of vegetation, an unusual displacement of soil, a few strands of red hair caught on a vine. The going was slow but steady, despite Blaze's urgings to move faster.

Occasionally Buju would have to cast ahead, sending the soldiers in two different directions until they found the next clue. Then they would pick up the trail again and move forward, closing in on their prey with every step. But at times the trail disappeared and Buju would be forced to make an educated guess, assessing the terrain and vegetation for the most likely direction of travel.

"Are you sure we're going the right way?" said Blaze as Buju stopped beside a fallen tree.

In answer to his question, the tracker picked up a blood-soaked wipe from the ground.

"One of them's injured!" exclaimed Dredd with glee.

No Mercy smiled to himself. Perhaps he had shot the boy after all.

"That'll slow them down," smirked Blaze.

Buju knelt and examined a print in the earth. "Leopard. Big one. Passed this way an hour ago."

The soldiers exchanged uneasy looks at the thought of a man-eater in their vicinity.

"We're not hunting leopard," Blaze snapped. "Just tell me where they headed next."

Buju scanned the undergrowth and noted a sharp change in direction. He pointed south.

The trail zigzagged through the jungle until the soldiers hit an animal track. Here, even No Mercy could spot the sign—a clear print of a sneaker heading upslope. Sensing they were drawing close to their quarry, the soldiers chambered their assault rifles. Unless the kids had walked through the night, they couldn't have made much more progress.

Cresting a small ridge, they stopped again. Buju studied the ground and surveyed the landscape.

"The trail's gone cold," he announced.

"What do you mean, *gone cold*?" snarled Blaze. "You claim to be the best tracker in Burundi. Find them!"

"It's harder to track someone on rocky terrain," Buju replied evenly.

Even through his mirrored sunglasses, Blaze's glare was searing. His right hand began to twitch and No Mercy took a cautious step back, recognizing the telltale signs of the man's legendary short fuse. Unless the tracker produced the goods very soon, there was little doubt that he'd be introduced to Blaze's machete and meet a gruesome end.

Farther down the hillside a wisp of smoke drifted above the canopy, catching one of the soldier's eyes.

"Look! There! A fire!"

6

Connor yawned, stretched and rubbed his eyes. After a night lying on the hard rock floor of the cave, his body felt stiff and sore. Amber was curled next to him, still asleep, her expression so peaceful that Connor had no desire to wake her, not with the sort of day that was ahead of them. He scratched his chest and sat up. Dawn had broken, the warming rays of the sun fingering their way into the cave. Birds warbled in the nearby treetops, and Connor heard the distinctive whooping of hyenas and the gruff roars of lions rising up from the savannah below.

Africa was coming to life.

The fire had burned out overnight, its ashes smoldering and leaving a smoky haze at the cave entrance. Connor gave himself another good scratch. His skin was feeling itchy, not surprising given the layers of grime, sweat and insect repellent. Then a painful nip on his leg caused him to wince. Glancing down, he discovered a massive ant with hooked jaws biting into his skin. He knocked it off with the back of his hand, but instantly it was replaced by three more equally monstrous ants. Then another six. As Connor went to dislodge them, he was met by a terrifying sight—a seething column of black driver ants swarming across the floor and crawling over him.

Connor jumped to his feet and brushed them away in a frenzy. But he was fighting a losing battle as the teeming mass surged into the cave and up his body.

Amber woke with a start. "What's wrong?" she asked as he slapped himself repeatedly.

"Ants!" cried Connor.

Seeing him leap around the cave like a wild cat, Amber began to giggle.

"It's *not* funny!" he said, ripping off his top to get at the ones now crawling under his shirt.

But Amber couldn't help herself. After all the horrors of the previous day, her laughter was a much-needed release, and she giggled uncontrollably—until she too saw the floor alive and rippling with the army of black ants.

"They're all over *me*!" she yelped, leaping up and shaking her arms and legs.

Connor had no idea if the ants were poisonous or not, but their bites hurt like crazy, leaving nasty red puncture wounds. Overrun by the horde, he realized they had to act fast.

"The pool!" he cried.

Running out of the cave, they both jumped into the water.

The coolness was an immediate relief and the ants were soon washed off, floating away like leaves with the current. Connor helped Amber remove the stubborn ones trapped in her long hair.

"All gone," he said, flicking the last into the water.

Amber turned back to him. As she did so, their arms became entwined and they ended up in an unexpected embrace. For a full second they simply stared at each other. Then she kissed him on the lips.

It was an impassioned, almost desperate kiss. And Connor abandoned himself to it, forgetting their situation, ignoring the danger they were in and simply relishing the moment of sweet delirium.

But his head quickly overruled his heart. He knew it was wrong, even as he continued to kiss her. Amber was vulnerable. Heartbroken from her recent breakup. Distraught at her parents' unknown fate. He guessed she was seeking comfort and security, confusing it with intimacy. And he couldn't blame her—the kiss was an escape for him too. But he knew from past experience that life-or-death situations intensified feelings, leading to developments that might not have occurred under ordinary circumstances. He reminded himself that he was her bodyguard. And as such, he couldn't cross that line into a personal relationship. Connor had made that mistake before, Charley having burst in on him and the US president's daughter at just such a moment. A second violation of the strict "no involvement with clients" rule would undoubtedly lead to his dismissal from Guardian.

Connor gently pulled away.

Amber looked up at him, confusion in her eyes.

"I shouldn't . . . I can't as your bodyguard." He glanced toward the cave, hoping that Henri hadn't witnessed their brief kiss. Then he was struck by the horrific realization that he was still in there with the ants. "Henri?" he called.

Amber spun around, their intimacy forgotten in an instant. *"Henri!"* she shouted, Connor having gotten no reply.

They scrambled out of the pool, both picturing Henri covered head to foot, the ants swarming into his nose and mouth, suffocating him. Reaching the cave entrance, they found the ferocious ants still on their relentless march across the cave floor but no Henri.

"He can't have gone far," said Connor, guessing her brother had also fled the tidal wave of insects. His eyes scanned the undergrowth, looking for any indication about which direction he might have run in.

"What if he's lost? Or he's been taken by a wild animal?" Amber said in a panic.

"Then we'll find him," Connor replied, grabbing his go-bag before it too fell prey to the ants.

"What *have* you two been up to?"

Startled, Connor and Amber spun to see Henri step from behind a bush. He stared at them—both dripping wet and Connor shirtless—with a knowing smirk on his lips.

Amber's face flushed red. Then, hiding her embarrassment behind anger, she demanded, "Where have *you* been? You had me worried sick!"

Henri held up his hands, filled with fresh berries. "Breakfast," he said.

Relieved just to see the boy safe, Connor said, "Next time don't wander off on your own."

"Sorry—but I thought you'd be hungry," he replied, offering Connor a handful.

Shaking out the last of the ants from his shirt before slipping it back on, Connor inspected the berries. "These could be poisonous."

"Don't worry, I saw a bunch of monkeys eating them," Henri explained, confidently popping one into his mouth.

Connor, overruling his caution, ate his share of the berries. Then he spread out the remains of the fire with his foot. As he covered it with dirt to ensure it was completely out, a final waft of smoke rose into the air.

7

"Fresh," said Buju, examining the remains of the berries dry-
ing on the rock. "But it could just be monkeys."

Blaze's stony expression suggested he wasn't convinced.
He nodded a silent order to the others to check the cave and
its surroundings. They quickly fanned out, their eyes to the
ground.

No Mercy spotted a patch of displaced earth. He kicked
away the dirt to reveal the ashes of a recent fire.

"It must be them," he called to Blaze.

One of the soldiers then found the charred skin of a
snake. He held it up for the others to see.

"They killed and ate a black mamba!" he exclaimed with
more than a little admiration.

Dredd wandered into the cave. His bare feet crunched on
the ground. It took a moment for his eyes to adjust to the
dimness before he spied the pile of leaves near the back wall.

"They slept in here," he informed Blaze.

Feeling a crawling sensation, he looked down to see a black mass swarming up his legs. His eyes widening in horror, Dredd bolted out of the cave.

"*Siafu! Siafu!*" he screamed, stamping his feet manically to dislodge the vicious driver ants as No Mercy and the other soldiers laughed.

"Dance, Dredd, dance!" taunted one of the men.

"Silence!" barked Blaze, indifferent to the boy's suffering. Turning his back on Dredd, he demanded of the tracker: "How long since the kids were here?"

Buju found a half-eaten berry, its skin dried out but its flesh still moist. "Ten minutes, maybe less."

"And which way did they go?"

The tracker's eyes surveyed the undergrowth. No stems were broken or leaves bruised. No foliage flattened. No footprints in the earth. That left only one obvious route.

"They're following the stream," he said.

Blaze unsheathed his machete, a grin on his lips. "Now the hunt really begins."

8

At first ankle-deep, the water was soon at knee-height, and on occasion, Connor, Amber and Henri found themselves wading up to their waists. The rocky bed made walking difficult, and as they followed the stream downhill, the current strengthened, threatening to sweep them away. However, without any clear paths through the dense undergrowth, Connor had determined that the stream was the quickest and most direct route out of the jungle.

The three of them trekked in silence, Connor taking the lead, Henri behind and Amber at the rear. She hadn't brought up the subject of their kiss and neither had he, but whenever he glanced back to check on them, she'd hold his gaze a moment before resolutely looking away. Connor couldn't tell whether this was through shyness, flirting or regret on her part. But there were far greater things to worry about than the consequences of a kiss.

Once they had navigated the stream down to the edge of

the jungle, they'd have to cross the open savannah, avoiding elephants, buffalos and lions while trying not to be spotted by rebel militia. To make matters worse, Connor had no map and only a vague idea of where the lodge was. If by some miracle they did manage to reach it safely, they still had to hope the facility was in government hands and that the comms radio was functional.

The sheer scale of the task ahead seemed impossible. But a phrase he'd once read in a book came to mind: *Don't try to eat an elephant for lunch.* The bizarre saying had confused him at first. Then his gran had explained that it meant any task the size of an elephant should be broken down into smaller, more manageable chunks. That way it wasn't such a daunting prospect. Applying the same principle to their current situation, Connor needed to focus on leading them safely through the jungle. That would be his first goal. Anything after that could wait.

The stream widened and Henri came up by his side.

"I never thought a safari would be like this," he said, attempting a smile that only revealed how scared he really was.

"Nor did I," admitted Connor. "But you'll have some story to tell your friends back home."

"Are we going to make it back home?" he asked, the simple question striking at the heart of their predicament.

Connor looked him squarely in the eye and, with as much confidence as he could muster, replied, "It's my job to protect you and your sister. I promise to get you both home safely."

Henri became thoughtful for a moment. "So, will you ask my sister out when we get back?"

Connor almost stumbled and fell into the water. "Um . . . I think you've got the wrong idea. We were just washing off the ants."

Henri gave him a sideways look that said *whatever,* then continued: "She likes you. I can tell."

Connor glanced over his shoulder. Amber was a little way back, concentrating on keeping her balance over the rocky streambed.

"It would be great if you were her boyfriend," enthused Henri. "Then we could hang out more. We could go to soccer matches together—"

Connor ruffled Henri's hair. "Enough of your matchmaking. Let's escape this jungle first, eh?"

As they were navigating around a small waterfall, they heard a distant voice cry out, *"Siafu! Siafu!"*

"Did you hear that?" said Amber, exchanging a fearful look with Connor.

Connor nodded. He recalled Gunner's words: *It doesn't matter whether you're a lion or a gazelle in this life; when the sun comes up, you'd better be running.*

They started running.

Clambering over the rocks and splashing through the shallows, they fled downstream. Although it was entirely possible the voice didn't belong to a rebel militia, Connor wasn't willing to take that gamble.

"Go! Go!" he urged, knowing they had to put significant distance between themselves and their pursuers if they were to have any chance of escaping capture.

But the water was slowing their progress. And tiring them too. Henri tripped and fell face-first into the stream. Connor dragged him to standing, pushing him ahead and alongside his sister. As the jungle thinned out and the waterway broadened, they took to the bank and headed across firm ground. Despite the spiny bushes clawing at their clothes, they were able to quicken their pace. But Connor realized they'd now be leaving clear tracks for the gunmen to follow.

Behind, they heard another shout. Closer this time.

Henri's breathing was tight and ragged, and he was struggling to keep up. When they finally reached the edge of the jungle, he was wheezing so badly that Connor thought he might collapse. Henri fumbled for his inhaler and took two desperate puffs.

"He can't keep this up much longer," panted Amber, leaning her brother against a tree to rest.

Looking out across the broad expanse of the savannah, Connor knew they had no hope of outrunning the gunmen. Certainly not with Henri's asthma. Ahead of them were miles of rolling hills and high grasses, interspersed with clumps of acacia trees, tangles of thornbushes and solitary baobabs rising up like sentinels from the red earth. In this terrain they'd be easy prey for any predator—particularly a group of well-armed militia.

"Perhaps we should just surrender?" Amber suggested. "I mean, why would they want to hurt us? Three kids. We're not a threat to anyone."

"The ambush we witnessed made us a threat," replied Connor. He glanced down at his father's knife and instantly dismissed any notion of making a stand against the gunmen.

Although they couldn't run, they could hide.

"The baobab," said Connor, pointing to one of the immense trees that dominated the savannah.

"What about it?" asked Amber.

"People rarely look up," explained Connor.

Immediately comprehending his plan, Amber urged Henri to his feet. Rushing over to the nearest baobab, a thirty-foot-tall gnarled specimen, Amber volunteered to climb the trunk first. The bark was knotty and offered lots of handholds, and her bouldering skills enabled her to pick out the fastest route. She ascended the trunk with the ease of a monkey. Once in the refuge of the lower boughs, more than twenty feet above the ground, she hung herself over the edge.

"Your turn, Henri," she said, beckoning him to join her.

Her brother took one look and shook his head. "I . . . can't . . . do it," he gasped. "I'm too . . . tired."

"Of course you can. With our help," said Connor, cupping his hands to give him a boost. "Now hurry—they can't be far off."

Snatching a last puff from his inhaler, Henri took hold of a groove in the bark and, with immense effort, began to haul himself up. While Amber guided her brother up the tree, Connor encouraged him from below. Exhausted and wheezing, Henri slowly inched his way up the trunk. Connor willed him to go faster, fully expecting to see the gunmen bearing down on them at any moment. But the tree line remained clear . . . for the time being, at least. What he did spot, however, caused him to turn and sprint back to the jungle.

"Where are you going?" Amber cried after him as she pulled her brother up the last few feet.

Connor didn't have time to explain. At the jungle edge, he used his knife to cut a leafy branch from a low-hanging tree. Then, retracing his steps to the baobab, he swept the dirt behind, obliterating all trace of their tracks. When he reached the base of the baobab, he flung the branch as far as he could before launching himself at the tree trunk. Clawing his way up, he was almost to the top when his foot slipped off a knot in the bark. He felt himself falling.

"I've got you!" said Amber, her hand clamping on to his wrist.

With gritted teeth and her muscles straining, she dragged him into the refuge of the boughs just as the gunmen burst from the jungle.

9

Peering from their hiding place, Connor was stunned to see the small lithe figure of Buju guiding the rebel soldiers onto the savannah. The tracker had seemed such a gentle and kindhearted man. Now it was evident that his quiet nature had been serving a duplicitous purpose. It also explained why the tracker had stopped the convoy in the middle of the riverbed. And why he had suddenly disappeared when the attack commenced. Buju was the one who'd betrayed the president, his entourage and the Barbier family.

The tracker was the traitor.

Connor watched as Buju quickly spotted the hewn branch on the tree, then knelt to examine the freshly swept earth— its color ever so slightly different from the surrounding soil. With a sinking feeling in his gut, Connor realized they'd never had a chance of eluding such a skilled tracker. His only surprise was that they hadn't been found sooner.

Five soldiers—three men and two boys, all armed with

rifles—stood beside Buju as he studied the ground. Connor recognized one of the boy soldiers by the black bandana on his head. He'd been the one firing with wild abandon into their Land Rover when they'd been forced to turn back at the trench. The other boy, in an oversized camo-jacket and red beret, toted a brand-new AK-47—and by the way he carried the weapon, it looked like he knew how to use it.

"Which way now?" asked a tall soldier in mirrored shades, his voice traveling clearly in the still, hot air of the savannah.

Buju began walking slowly toward the baobab, following the traces of the swept track. Connor's heart was in his mouth, and his hand went to his knife in readiness. Amber and Henri clung on beside him, the boy's labored breathing whistling in his ear. As the soldiers drew ever nearer, the three of them sank farther into the hollow of the boughs, in a futile last attempt to stay hidden.

Buju knelt to examine the earth once more.

"It's hard to tell," he replied. "They've wiped their tracks."

The rebel in the mirrored shades swore, kicking at the dirt with a heavy black boot.

"Spread out!" he ordered his soldiers. "They can't be far away."

"Wait!" said Buju, holding up his hand. "You'll disturb any signs they might have left."

Standing, he scanned the terrain, his gaze passing over the long grasses, the baobab tree, the tangle of bushes . . .

then flicking back again to the baobab. Connor felt like a mouse caught in the deadly sights of a hawk.

It was all over. There was nowhere to run. No chance of fighting. No hope of hiding.

"What is it, Buju?" asked the rebel.

Buju's gaze immediately dropped to the discarded branch, near to the base of the baobab.

"Have you seen something?" demanded the rebel, his mirrored glasses glinting in the sun as he looked sharply around. "Where are they?"

"This way," said Buju, walking purposefully on.

10

Connor peered from the bough as Buju proceeded to lead the soldiers *away* from their baobab tree and into an acacia thicket. Connor was utterly baffled, until he saw the gleam of a large machete, its tip pressed against the small of the tracker's back.

"Buju looked straight at us!" exclaimed Amber under her breath. "He *knew* we were hiding here."

Connor nodded solemnly. "That's why he went the other way."

"He's on our side?" questioned Henri, no longer wheezing so badly.

"Apparently so. By the looks of it, he's being forced to track us."

Cautiously sitting up, Connor peered in the direction the rebels had gone. Amid the tall grasses on the next rise, he spotted the distinctive red beret of the boy soldier. They were still heading away from them. But how long Buju could keep up the pretense of following a false trail was anyone's guess. And Connor didn't think the rebel with mirrored sunglasses was likely to be taken for a fool.

"Let's move while we can," he said. In the distance he could see the ridge upon which the lodge was located. Gloriously lit by the morning sun, it offered the promise of a safe haven. But between them and the ridge stretched the open savannah populated by herds of grazing zebra, kudu and antelope, along with the unseen threat of lion, leopard and cheetah lurking in the undergrowth.

This assignment should be a walk in the park for you, Charley had said.

Some walk this is turning out to be, thought Connor as he took a bearing on the ridge with his compass watch.

Swinging his legs off the bough and onto the trunk, he clambered down from the baobab, followed by Henri and Amber. Once on the ground, they lost sight of their destination, but relying on the compass, they set off due south.

"How long do you think it will take us now?" asked Amber with an anxious glance at her asthmatic brother.

"Depends how fast we can walk," Connor replied as they headed up a rise, winding between clumps of bushes and trees. "Four, maybe five hours."

Above their heads yellow weaverbirds swooped, catching tiny insects disturbed from the grass by their feet. The bush hummed with life, and the sun, blazing in the powder-blue sky, was already sending ripples of heat up from the ground. Connor wiped the sweat from his brow as they continued to climb.

"Do we have any water?" asked Henri, his voice tight and hoarse.

"Sure," said Connor, having filled the bottle back at the cave. Stopping, he unscrewed the cap, inserted the LifeStraw and passed the bottle to Henri. "Only take a few sips," he advised. "It might be some time before we reach the river and can refill."

Henri grimaced at the taste of the warm, chemically treated water. "What I'd do for an ice-cold can of Coke," he said, sighing.

As he sucked on the straw, Amber said quietly, "It's good that Buju's still alive."

Connor nodded, his eyes scanning the scrub for any sign of predators. The knowledge Gunner had imparted about the African wildlife made him more aware than ever of the constant danger surrounding them.

"Probably means our parents are okay too," continued Amber, phrasing it more as a question than a statement.

"Yes, it seems likely," agreed Connor, taking the water bottle back from Henri. As long as Laurent and Cerise served a purpose for the rebels, then Connor reasoned they might still be alive—if only as hostages to demand a ransom from the French government. It was a slender hope but a credible one.

As they approached the top of the rise, a gunshot echoed across the plain.

"Down!" cried Connor, pushing both Henri and Amber to the ground.

There was more gunfire—but at a distance. Retrieving the binoculars from his pack, Connor rose to his knees and searched for the source of the shots. But he didn't need binoculars to realize what was happening.

11

Buju fled through the bush, crouching down low as bullets tore up the undergrowth around him. The threat of his own torture and death had impelled him to track the children. But he hadn't been able to betray them. Not when he knew the horrendous fate that awaited them.

Of course he'd spotted the three youngsters in the baobab tree. To a tracker, it was the most obvious place to hide. And the red hair of the French brother and sister was like a beacon in the bush. But when he'd seen them tucked in the hollow of the lower boughs, it wasn't their faces he saw but the faces of his own children. He realized that whatever the risks to his own life, he couldn't be responsible for their capture. No parent on earth would wish their offspring to suffer at the hands of these cruel rebel soldiers.

After leading the gunmen away from their quarry, he'd kept up the pretense of following a live trail. But it wasn't long before Blaze began to suspect something. That's when he'd made the stupid mistake of fabricating a sign—to convince the rebel they were still on the right track. Asking some of the soldiers to cast ahead, he'd snapped a plant stem when he thought no one was looking. Then a minute later he'd announced its discovery and the direction in which the children were supposedly fleeing.

But the boy soldier No Mercy had spotted his deception and declared him a liar.

That was the moment he ran for his life.

"Don't let that snake get away!" Blaze snarled over the ferocious blasts of AK-47s.

Like a bolting rabbit, Buju zigzagged through bushes. If he could reach the cover of the jungle, he might have a chance of losing them among the trees. But blood flowed freely from the gash across his back where Blaze had slashed at him when he'd fled. He could feel it dripping off him, leaving a bright red trail in his wake.

The soldiers raced after him, their guns blazing.

A bullet clipped his shoulder, knocking him to the ground. Buju got up, staggering, before another shot pierced his thigh. He stumbled on, the tree line almost within reach, until he felt a rock-hard strike to his back as a round punctured his right lung. He was crawling now, the jungle only feet away from him . . .

Suddenly all was calm, the heavy thunder of gunfire fading and the sounds of the savannah returning. He could hear the sawlike buzz of cicadas in the grass. The warbling of weaverbirds in the trees. The braying of zebra, and somewhere in the distance, the mighty roar of a lion. Buju saw his lifeblood seeping into the red earth and grasped the rich soil between his fingers for one last time, savoring its warmth and comfort.

Then the tracker was wrenched from his dying peace as Blaze planted a foot on his back, seized the curls of his hair and jerked his head back.

Pressing the edge of his machete against Buju's throat, he demanded, "Which way did the children *really* go?"

Buju gasped in pain. "They're miles . . . away . . . by now."

"You lie. I know we were on the right track."

"You'll never find them . . . without me," wheezed Buju.

"We'll see about that," said Blaze and drew the blade sharply across Buju's throat.

Blood sprayed into the red earth, and the tracker fell still. Flicking the gore off his machete, then wiping it on the dead tracker's shirt, Blaze stood and surveyed the savannah.

"Double back to the baobab tree," he told his gang of misfit soldiers. "That's where we lost their trail."

As No Mercy obeyed Blaze's order, he thought he caught a gleam of reflected sunlight on the rise. A second glint convinced him that he hadn't been mistaken.

12

Sickened at the sight of Buju's slaughter, Connor lowered his binoculars. He'd seen the boy soldier with the red beret point in their direction and wondered how on earth they'd been spotted so quickly. Buju no longer knew where they were, so he couldn't have betrayed them. Then, as he stuffed the binoculars back into his go-bag, Connor cursed his stupidity—he'd been looking due east, so the sunlight would have reflected off the lenses.

"What's going on?" asked Amber, still lying prone in the dirt beside her brother.

"Buju's just been killed," he explained.

"My God, no!" The blood visibly drained from her face as the hope she'd held for her parents' survival died along with Buju.

Connor dragged the two of them to their feet. "The gunmen are coming this way. We need to move fast!"

Staying low, they kept to the cover of the bushes as much

as they could. Without Buju to guide the rebels, Connor hoped the soldiers would be slower to track them. So long as the three of them stayed out of sight, they might still have a slim chance of evading their pursuers.

As they crested the rise, the savannah once again opened out before them, mounds of granite boulders breaking up the terrain between strips of dense undergrowth and islands of flat-top trees. In the distance the land smoothed out into a grassy plain where the Ruvubu River wound like a glistening python, dividing the valley in two. Until now Connor hadn't given any consideration to how they'd cross that wide stretch of waterway . . . *if* they even got that far.

He risked a quick glance back and spotted the red beret racing through the long grass and bushes toward them.

"Keep going," Connor urged, directing Amber and Henri downslope.

Running as fast as Henri's asthma would allow, they followed an animal trail across the savannah and into a dense thicket. Emerging at the other side, Amber came to an abrupt halt, Henri and Connor almost running into the back of her before they also froze.

Up ahead of them a zebra was being ripped apart in a feeding frenzy by a pack of spotted hyenas. Their powerful jaws snapping, their fur stained with blood, they squabbled over the kill, cackling and giggling.

The lower-ranked hyenas, pushed out by the dominant

females, instantly turned their attention to the human intruders. Staring at their newfound prey with dark, hungry eyes, they bared their teeth, drool dripping from their ravenous mouths. One by one, the other hyenas fell silent as they became aware of the presence of Connor, Amber and Henri.

Faced by such a fearsome pack of wild animals, it took all Connor's willpower not to simply turn and flee. But he knew from Gunner's advice that to do such a thing would trigger the hunting instinct.

"*Back away,*" he whispered, trying to keep the panic out of his voice. "*Slowly.*"

Amber managed the slightest of nods in acknowledgment. They retreated a step at a time, drawing back into the cover of the thicket. The hyenas advanced in slow, deliberate paces, determined to keep their quarry in sight. Henri glanced behind to see where he was walking, and a large hyena with a ripped ear stealthily closed the gap.

"*Don't* take your eyes off them," Connor warned. "As soon as you do, they'll attack."

They were almost concealed within the thicket when the matriarch of the clan let out a haunting *whoop* and all of a sudden the hyenas launched themselves. Survival instinct overruling any ranger's advice, Amber, Henri and Connor ran for their lives. They fled through the bush, not caring as the thorns of a wait-a-while tore at their clothes and ripped their skin. Maniacal giggles and growls pursued them on all sides, and Connor caught flashes of sandy-brown hair, black snouts and muscular forelegs closing in.

The three of them broke from the thicket and into the long grass. The hyenas matched them pace for pace, boxing them in but not yet attacking. For a brief second Connor wondered why—then realized the pack was simply tiring them out to make the kill easier.

"The trees!" cried Amber, pointing to a copse of acacia farther up the slope.

Connor saw them too and, recalling Gunner saying that hyenas couldn't climb, shepherded his two Principals toward the promised sanctuary of the trees. But they were forced to change direction when a huge snarling hyena blocked their path. They ran across a slope, skirting around a huge pile of boulders as they looked for another way through. Henri was wheezing heavily by now, his face pale with the exertion.

"Up there," Connor shouted, spotting a narrow gully between the massive boulders.

Taking advantage of a gap in the pack, he led the way to the opening. But the moment they reached it, the hyena with the ripped ear lunged at Henri. Panicking, Henri fled in the opposite direction and was soon lost from sight in the tall grass. Connor could hear the pack whooping and howling as they hunted down the youngest and weakest of their chosen prey.

"We have to save him!" Amber cried.

But the hunt wasn't over for them either. Two hyenas were pursuing them up the gully. Then another appeared at the top. Trapped, Connor searched frantically for a different escape route.

"In there," he said, spotting a narrow gap between two gigantic boulders.

"It's too small," cried Amber.

Faced with no alternative and the hyenas bearing down on them, Connor shoved her toward the hole. Slender as she was, Amber still struggled to wiggle through. He tossed in his go-bag, then sucked in his chest as he scrambled after her. But he got stuck halfway, the rocks seeming to press down on him, crushing the breath from his body. He could hear the hyenas bounding toward his exposed flailing legs. Amber, who'd managed to crawl into a little hollow beneath the boulders, tugged frantically on his arms. With a final desperate squirm, Connor scraped through the suffocating gap, just as the hyenas' jaws snapped at his disappearing feet.

13

Connor and Amber lay pressed against each other in the cramped confines of the hollow. The three hyenas snarled and scratched at the entrance, frustrated at being so close yet unable to sink their teeth into their prey.

"What now?" shrieked Amber as she desperately tried to avoid their probing forepaws.

"Don't worry—they can't get to us," said Connor, glad the hyenas' heavily built shoulders barred them entering any farther.

"But we have to get out! We need to rescue Henri!"

A wave of guilt consumed Connor. He dared not think about the poor boy's fate. But how could he be expected to protect *two* individuals at once? Especially against a pack of hunting hyenas. He and Amber had barely escaped with their own lives—and they weren't out of trouble yet.

"We'll find him," said Connor, hearing the hollowness in his own promise.

"Not before those hyenas have finished him off!"

Amber began to sob—fear, shock and grief all welling up at once. "Why did we ever come to Burundi? *Why?* This is a living hell! My parents murdered . . . my brother eaten alive . . . I—I . . ."

Connor drew Amber close, letting her cry herself out. The horrors of the past twenty-four hours were enough to break anyone. In fact, he was surprised that she'd held it together for so long. Despite all his hostile environment training, even he was on the point of snapping. Connor had thought his previous two missions would have prepared him for any eventuality. But it dawned on him that *nothing* could have prepared him for Africa. Violent ambushes, murdering gunmen, deadly snakes and man-eating hyenas—Operation Lionheart had been woefully underestimated in terms of threat level and required security support. His only comfort was that he'd failed to call in at two consecutive report times. Alarm bells would be ringing back at HQ and Charley would be investigating the problem, establishing the reason for the communication breakdown and implementing a search-and-rescue operation.

They just had to stay alive until rescue arrived.

Amber's sobbing faded and Connor became aware that the hyenas had gone quiet too.

"Do you think they've given up?" whispered Amber, her head still resting against his chest.

Shifting closer to the entrance, Connor peered out. The sun glared down on an empty patch of scrub and bare rock, a flurry of paw marks in the dirt the only evidence that hyenas had been there at all.

"Maybe," he replied, edging farther out for a better look.

Suddenly he was nose to nose with a snarling hyena. Connor jerked back into the hollow. The hyena *whooped* and began to dig more furiously than before.

"I guess that answers your question," said Connor, shocked at the calculating nature of the animals. He'd spotted the other two hyenas patiently waiting on a boulder, ready to pounce as soon as they emerged.

Connor searched frantically for another way out of their tiny refuge, but they were well and truly stuck between a rock and a hard place. The hollow backed up against another immovable boulder, and any openings were barely large enough for a rabbit to fit through. Desperation had driven him to think this gap offered some sort of escape. Now it was destined to be their grave.

The hyena's claws continued to rip at the ground, the entrance hole growing by the minute. Soon the opening would be large enough for its shoulders to pass through and its jaws to enter the hollow and rip them limb from limb.

Amber began her own frantic attempt at digging, using a stone to gouge out a hole behind her. As dirt rained in on them, Connor realized she had entered into a race that they were guaranteed to lose. He drew his father's knife. He'd have to kill the beast before it dug its way in first. But the broad bony skull looked impenetrable, even with a survival knife, and the sharp-pointed teeth appeared fearsome weapons to overcome. It would be a bloody and fraught fight to the death for one of them.

As Connor steeled himself for an attack, a gunshot rang out, startling the hyena, and it stopped digging. More heavy gunfire caused it to turn tail and flee. Connor and Amber exchanged a glance, at once relieved yet fearful of what was to come next.

They heard the sound of heavy boots crunching in the dirt.

"I saw them enter the gully, Blaze," said a boy's voice.

"Then where are they?" growled a deeper voice that Connor recognized as belonging to the rebel with mirrored sunglasses.

A shadow passed across the hollow's entrance, and Connor spotted a pair of black boots and the bare feet of a boy worryingly close to their hiding place.

"Maybe they escaped."

Suddenly Amber's body went rigid. Disturbed by her earlier digging, a small oil-black spider with a bulbous abdomen had emerged and was crawling across her arm. Realizing Amber was about to scream and give away their location, Connor clamped a hand over her mouth. Her eyes grew wide with sheer terror as the eight-legged arachnid crept up her arm and toward her neck.

"Did you *see* them escape?" Blaze questioned.

"No," replied the boy.

As the spider reached her shoulder, Connor noticed a distinctive red hourglass marking on its underbelly. At once he felt Amber's paralyzing fear seep into his own bones.

"Then search the gully, top to bottom," ordered Blaze. "Leave no stone unturned."

14

The black widow continued its slow yet deliberate journey up Amber's neck. Neither Connor nor Amber could move, both held captive by the venomous spider as it probed her cheek with its forelegs, its multiple eyes glistening in the hollow's dim light.

Amber closed her own eyes as her worst nightmare stared directly at her. Connor could feel a cold sweat break out on her skin as the spider crawled across her face. Its legs brushed against his fingers, which were still clamped over Amber's mouth. But he dared not knock the black widow off. They had nowhere to go and a single bite from such a spider could inject a lethal neurotoxin, resulting in burning pain, vomiting, swelling and even death.

In the gully, the soldiers were working their way down, searching every nook and crevice. Connor could hear them getting closer with each passing second. Amber was now as pale as death, the spider passing across her right eyelid. She twitched in panic and the black widow stopped, probing her soft skin with its two front legs.

Footsteps approached their hollow, the entrance darkening as a soldier bent down to look inside. Then a second gunshot went off, swiftly followed by several more blasts.

"Over here!" came a distant cry.

The shadow disappeared from their entrance, the crunch of feet on earth rapidly receding. But neither Connor nor Amber could risk moving. The black widow was now painstakingly making its way through her tangle of red hair. Connor prayed the creature wouldn't decide to make a nest there. Amber had her eyes fixed on his, utter desperation filling them as she heard the whisper of the eight-legged creature pass her ear.

After what seemed an eternity, the spider crawled out onto the rock and disappeared into a dark fissure.

"It's gone," whispered Connor.

As if woken from a trance, Amber bolted for the entrance.

"No!" hissed Connor. "They might still be out there."

But Amber was paying him no heed. She scrambled out of the hollow and into the sunlight. Left with no other choice, Connor shoved his go-bag through the opening and followed close behind. He found Amber sitting on a rock, panting rapidly, her hands trembling. Connor quickly scanned the gully. Thankfully there were no soldiers or hyenas in sight. He knelt before Amber.

"Are you okay?" he asked.

Still in post-phobic shock, her eyes glassy and unfocused, she didn't reply. But the color in her cheeks seemed to be slowly returning. Connor touched her arm and she almost leaped out of her skin.

"It's all right," soothed Connor. "You're safe now."

"Safe?" said Amber, staring at him incredulously, then waving her hand at the surrounding savannah. "You call *this* safe?"

She stood and began striding down the gully. Connor grabbed her arm.

"Let me go," she demanded with a fierce glare at him.

"But that's the direction the gunmen went," argued Connor.

"It's also the way my brother went," she replied, shaking herself free from his grip and dashing out of the gully.

15

Shouldering his go-bag, Connor raced after her, expecting at any moment to run straight into the rebel soldiers . . . or the open jaws of a bloodthirsty hyena. He almost lost sight of Amber among the tall grasses but finally caught up with her kneeling at the base of a small acacia tree. Henri's inhaler was lying discarded in the dirt beside a pool of sticky blood, a cloud of flies buzzing over its surface. Connor felt his heart sink. They were too late.

"Have you . . . found him?" he asked, fearing the hyenas had torn the boy apart.

"It isn't his blood," said Amber quietly as she retrieved the inhaler. She indicated a dead hyena sprawled on the ground behind the tree, its belly exploded open by a high-caliber round. "My brother must have reached this tree. He was safe. He escaped the hyenas, but"—she looked up at him, her eyes rimmed red with tears—"not the gunmen."

They'd both heard the repeated blasts of gunfire and

the rebel soldier shout out. However, that didn't necessarily mean Henri had been shot. The evidence suggested the rebel had saved her brother from being eaten by the hyenas. That was surely a good sign. But what had happened to Henri afterward? That was the question.

Was he injured? Had he escaped? Or had the soldier captured him?

From a nearby bush came a pained high-pitched cry.

"Henri?" called Amber in desperate hope.

They rushed over only to discover a wounded hyena. It lifted its head at their approach, revealing a torn ear, and snarled at them. Bullets had reduced the animal's hindquarters to a bloody, furry mess, yet the beast still clung to life. It lunged at them with its forepaws, its jaws snapping in agonized torment. Even as it was dying, the hyena seemed determined to kill them.

Connor and Amber backed cautiously away.

"We *have* to find Henri," insisted Amber.

"Our best hope is to reach the lodge and call for backup."

"No," said Amber firmly. "I won't leave my brother alone in this hellhole. I need to find out what's happened to him."

It was a catch-22 situation. Connor couldn't abandon Henri to his fate. Yet he couldn't lead Amber into further danger. She was the one Principal left under his protection. That made her his priority. *Or did it?* They were both equally important. But should he risk one to save the other? It was a gamble that could result in him losing *both* Principals, as well as his own life.

Hearing a rustle in the grass behind him, Connor spun to confront a rebel soldier emerging from the bushes. Before the man could level his AK-47, Connor hip-shoved Amber to one side, sending her flying into the cover of the tree. Then he launched himself at the soldier, taking three running steps to add power to his flying side-kick. The soldier, completely unprepared for the speed and suddenness of the attack, was struck in the chest. The technique, a specialty of Connor's in kickboxing matches, impacted so hard that Connor heard a rib crack as the soldier was knocked off his feet. The man tumbled backward into the heart of a wait-a-while bush and was instantly ensnared. Scrambling to seize hold of his AK-47, he only entangled himself further until the bush had wrapped around him like a ball of barbed wire. Helpless in its clutches, bleeding from multiple cuts and wheezing from a broken rib, the soldier cried out for help.

Connor turned to Amber to make their escape, but before they could, the barrel of a gun was pressed into the small of his back.

"Don't m—"

Not waiting for the rebel to finish his sentence, Connor pivoted on the spot, knocking the barrel aside with his elbow, and struck full force with a one-inch push to the chest. The modified palm strike not only smashed the solar plexus, winding his attacker, but also sent him flying several feet back. A burst of rapid gunfire filled the air, bullets shooting off in all directions as the rebel crashed down hard onto the ground. Connor dropped to one knee while Amber cowered behind the protection of the tree trunk, splinters of bark flying.

For the first time Connor got a good look at his attacker. It was the boy soldier with the black bandana, the name DREDD etched in white across the front. He wore the same dead-eyed gaze as when he'd shot at their Land Rover, and his right ear was missing, as if it had been hacked off by a machete. The boy was slightly smaller than Connor but, hardened from a life of warfare in the jungle, he was already rising to his feet. Connor couldn't let that happen. He rushed over and kicked the assault rifle from his grasp.

Trained only in fist brawls, Dredd bulldozed headfirst into Connor's stomach. The tactic, inelegant but effective, knocked the wind out of Connor, and they both tumbled to the ground. Dredd rose first, pinning Connor's arms with his knees, then pummeled him with his fists. Connor's head rang as he was pounded with knuckles hard as iron. Somewhere far off he heard Amber cry out his name and the howl of the wounded hyena. Connor bucked and arched his back, trying to dislodge Dredd from his dominant position as a particularly vicious strike split his left eyebrow. Blood pouring into his eye, Connor's vision became blurred. If he didn't do something soon, he'd be beaten to death.

He tried to reach for his knife, but the handle was caught beneath him and his arms were still pinned.

Come on, hotshot. The round's not over yet.

Ling's ringside taunts filled his head. Their matches had not only toughened him up but also taught him a trick or two. One of her favored techniques was to attack nerve points—*kyusho-jitsu*—enabling her to disable limbs, inflict extreme pain and break down the body's ability to fight, nerve by nerve.

Dredd stopped battering him with his fists, but only to grab a large stone. Through the red filter of his vision, Connor saw the boy lift it high above his head. Realizing with horror that a single strike would be the end of him, Connor reached for the *yako* point—halfway up the boy's inner thigh. He pinched and twisted the nerve near the skin's surface.

Dredd leaped off him with a high-pitched yelp of pain, then a moment later began screaming. Dazed and bloodied, Connor crawled away. Even he was amazed that the nerve point was so effective. Then he saw that the boy had rolled into the wounded hyena's reach. Its jaws had clamped around Dredd's upper arm, which it was now ravaging between its teeth. In agonized panic, Dredd battered at the hyena's head with the rock. But he was having little effect on the enraged animal.

Connor staggered to his feet, seizing their opportunity to escape.

"Aidez-moi!" cried the boy soldier, his attack on the hyena weakening as the animal gnawed on his arm. *"Help! Please!"*

Despite Amber being his number one priority, Connor couldn't leave the boy to be ripped to shreds. It was too horrific a death, even for someone who'd just tried to kill him. The boy's AK-47 lay in the dirt beside Connor. Snatching up the assault rifle, its weight even heavier than he'd anticipated, he lined up the sights and pulled the trigger. The AK-47 roared, its butt hammering into his shoulder, the recoil of automatic fire almost knocking him over. Bullets ripped up the ground as he battled to keep control of the powerful weapon. The hyena, its jaws still clenched around the mauled arm, let out a pained whimper, then went limp. Dredd collapsed back onto the earth, groaning in pain but alive.

"Let's go," said Connor, running over to Amber. He could hear the other rebels, alerted by the gunfire, crashing through the bush toward them.

"But what about Henri?" she asked as he dragged her into the long grass.

"We'll never find him if we're dead."

16

Barely knowing in which direction they were headed, Connor's only goal was to evade the gunmen. Keeping a firm grasp of Amber's hand, he weaved a path through the disorienting clumps of bushes and trees. As he ran, the AK-47 thumped painfully against his hip. Cumbersome and heavy, the weapon was slowing him down. But he rejected the idea of discarding it. The rifle was their only serious means of defense.

The shouts of the rebel soldiers continued to pursue them through the bush, drawing ever closer. Connor stopped, shouldered the rifle and fired several warning shots into the trees.

Clamping her hands over her ears to muffle the gun's thunderous blasts, Amber cried, "You've just given our position away!"

Connor nodded. "But now they know we have a weapon

too. That should make them more cautious about following us. And, ideally, slow them down."

Avoiding the obvious trail that lay before them, Connor checked his compass watch and altered direction, heading at right angles through the bush. The sun was glaringly hot, and his throat felt parched and clogged with dust. Amber was also panting hard, but he dared not stop again, however much a drink might revive them. As they scaled a steep rocky slope, Amber stumbled and Connor had to drág her upright. The constant running was beginning to take its toll on both of them. Their meager breakfast of berries had been barely enough to satisfy their hunger, let alone sustain them. Now they were running on empty, only adrenaline and fear fueling their flight.

They burst through a copse of trees and disturbed a group of dik-diks feeding on the brush. The tiny fawn-colored antelopes bounded away, whistling a high-pitched *zick-zick* in alarm. Connor knew the soldiers would be onto them again. To make matters worse, the ridge had flattened out into a grassy plateau, leaving them dangerously exposed. As they raced across the open ground, Connor heard the sound of rushing water. It grew louder with every step until it became a mighty roar. All of a sudden they found themselves teetering on the brink of a barren rock ledge. A billowing curtain of white water cascaded some hundred feet straight down to form one of the primary tributaries that fed the Ruvubu River. A fine mist hung in the air, catching rainbows of glistening sunlight.

Connor cursed their bad luck. The overhang was little more than a picturesque dead end for them. They'd have to double back and find an alternative route to the plain.

"We could climb down," suggested Amber, peering over the ledge at the sheer rock face. Connor took one glance at the dizzying drop and the slick, treacherous stone and felt his stomach lurch.

"Not if I were you," said a rough voice. "This is Dead Woman's Fall."

The two of them spun around to find Blaze standing behind them, his shaven head glistening with sweat from the chase. A moment later the boy soldier with the red beret appeared, breathing hard, gun in hand. Connor immediately leveled his own AK-47 at Blaze.

"The Batwa tribe used to throw women suspected of witchcraft from this ledge," the rebel explained, unperturbed by the gun pointing at his chest. "Any woman who survived the fall was declared a witch and put to death." He thumbed the handle of his machete on his hip as he slowly advanced on them. "But most didn't survive, and the few who did were almost always eaten alive by the crocodiles waiting at the bottom."

Blaze smirked at their horrified expressions as they were forced to retreat to the very lip of the precipitous drop. Connor thrust the AK-47's barrel at the rebel. "Stay back!"

Blaze held up his hands in mock surrender. "Whatever you say, chief."

"What have you done with Henri?" demanded Amber.

Blaze's eyes raked over her. "That little redheaded kid? I'm afraid a hyena got its teeth into him. He was screaming like a stuck pig, so I put the boy out of his misery." The rebel patted the machete, its metal blade smeared with fresh blood.

"NO!" gasped Amber, her legs giving way beneath her.

"I'm so sorry," said Blaze with false sincerity as he edged closer. "I can understand how upsetting this m—"

"This is your last warning," cut in Connor. "One more step and you're a dead man."

Blaze cocked his head to one side and studied Connor's face intently. "Unlike No Mercy here"—his eyes flicked to the boy soldier—"you're no killer."

"You want to test that theory?" said Connor, his finger primed on the trigger. But deep down he too questioned his ability to shoot a man at point-blank range.

Blaze shrugged indifferently. "Well, if you had the killer instinct, you'd have let Dredd die. I certainly would have."

The rebel took another brazen step forward.

Connor pulled the trigger.

There was just a dry *click*. He squeezed again. Nothing. The AK-47 had jammed.

Laughing, Blaze unsheathed his machete and pointed its tip at Connor. "Nowhere to run now, chief!"

Connor hurled the useless rifle at the rebel. Then, grabbing hold of Amber, he jumped off the ledge.

17

"Connor is probably enjoying himself too much to reply," said Jason, his feet propped up on the desk in Alpha team's operations room as Charley attempted to call Connor's phone for the third time that morning. "If I were him, I'd be relaxing in a private pool, chatting with that French girl."

Charley bristled at the suggestion and Ling flung a pen at Jason's head.

"I was only joking!" cried Jason, ducking just in time.

Ling shot him a furious glare, then turned to Charley. "Remember, communication's pretty nonexistent within the park. It's possible he doesn't have a signal."

"I know, but it's not like Connor to miss an evening *and* a morning report-in. I can't contact him on his phone or get through to the lodge. I can't even locate his phone using the GPS app," she explained, pointing to the digital map of Burundi displayed on her computer screen. "That's over twelve hours without official contact. It's time we raised the alert."

"Aren't you being a little hasty?" said Richie, munching on a bowl of cornflakes. "He's probably been asleep most of that time. And it's not as if they're in the middle of a war zone. He's on a safari vacation, for heaven's sake!"

Jason nodded in agreement. "Connor would use the SOS app if he was in real trouble."

"If he's in *real* trouble, he might not be able to use the SOS app," Charley argued.

"Try the lodge one more time," suggested Ling. "Then we'll go to the colonel."

Charley picked up the phone and dialed. The connection failed as before. She tried again. There was a distant echoing ring. Her hand clasped the receiver tighter. After eight rings, the call was picked up.

"*Bonjour, Ruvubu Safari Lodge. C'est Yasmina qui parle. Comment puis-je vous aider?*"

The line was poor, but the voice was clear enough to make out.

"*Parlez-vous anglais?*" asked Charley, switching to speaker-phone so the others could hear.

After a slight delay, the voice answered, "Of course. How can I help?"

"I would like to speak to one of your guests. Connor Reeves? He's staying with the Barbier family."

There was a longer pause. "I'm sorry. They're currently on a bush safari. Would you like to leave a message?"

"Yes, please tell him his sister Charley called and to get in touch as soon as possible."

"Certainly. Have a good day." The line went dead.

"See!" said Jason, leaning back in his chair, his hands behind his head. "Told you there was nothing to worry about."

18

The lodge receptionist put down the telephone with a trembling hand.

"Well done, Yasmina," said General Pascal, stroking the young lady's cheek with the barrel of his Glock 17. She shuddered as he then traced a line down her slender neck. "Now get me a drink," he ordered, waving the pistol toward the lounge area. "Whisky. The finest."

The receptionist hurried to the bar as the general strolled in after her.

"My apologies for keeping you waiting," he said. "But we need to keep up appearances to the outside world. At least for the time being."

Mr. Gray turned from studying the leopard-skin shield and spears on the wall to face the general. "By all accounts you're ahead of schedule. I must confess even I was surprised at the swiftness of your coup."

"You have to seize life before it seizes you!" General Pascal told him, laughing. "But there's more work to be done. The head may have been cut off the chicken, but the body still runs around."

"Is that why you need the heavy artillery so quickly?"

The general nodded as the receptionist gingerly stepped over the dead body of the barman, the victim's blood still pooling on the parquet floor, and brought over his whisky. "Would you like a drink, Mr. Gray?" asked the general.

"Sparkling water. No ice."

General Pascal frowned. "I'd have thought a man in your line of work would drink something stronger."

"And I'd have thought a man of your strength wouldn't need to drink anything stronger," Mr. Gray replied coolly.

Their eyes locked and the receptionist took a nervous step back, sensing a change in atmosphere, as if two prowling lions were in the room. Then the general broke into an affable grin at his guest's sharp retort. He waved the receptionist away.

"Unfortunately, we still have the army to fight before we can take control of this country. But I'm confident of our imminent victory. An army of sheep"—he glanced in the direction of a boy soldier standing guard on the open-air veranda—"led by a lion can defeat an army of lions led by a sheep. And, I can assure you, the commander in chief of the Burundian army is but a lamb compared with me."

The receptionist served the sparkling water and Mr. Gray

took a measured sip. "Equilibrium can supply the weapons you require at short notice," he said. "But we'll need payment up front."

"No problem," replied the general, downing his whisky in one swift gulp. "Come with me to the mine and take your pick of the diamonds. But first I must introduce you to the man who helped arrange President Bagaza's sudden demise."

19

Whistling past the rock face, Connor and Amber barely had time to contemplate the drop before they plunged into the bottom of Dead Woman's Fall three seconds later. Hitting the river's surface at over fifty miles an hour, Amber was torn from Connor's grip and lost amid the churning waters.

The swirling current pinned Connor beneath its surface, where he was spun, twisted and battered against submerged rocks, knocking the wind out of him. He kicked wildly with his legs, desperate for air, but the white water blinded him, and he was deafened by its thunderous roar. Totally disoriented, Connor soon gave up all hope of escaping the watery clutches of Dead Woman's Fall. Blaze hadn't been lying when he'd said that few people survived the Batwa tribe's ordeal.

With his lungs burning for oxygen, Connor felt his body involuntarily start to suck in water. As he fought the overwhelming urge, his feet briefly touched down on the riverbed. Calling on the last of his strength, he thrust himself upward. A moment later he broke the surface and snatched a lungful of glorious air . . . before being swamped by another rush of water and forced under again.

The torrent roiled and seethed around him, but glimmers of sunlight guided him back to the surface now. Coughing and spluttering, Connor swam with the current, struggling to get his breath back and control his panic. The river's rapids blasted him like fire hoses from all directions, mere seconds before another wall of white water engulfed him. Then he was spat out again, bounced off a rock and borne relentlessly through the next series of rapids.

Weakening with every wave and collision, Connor was on the point of drowning when the torrent suddenly eased and the rumble of Dead Woman's Fall began to recede into the distance. He floated limply on his back, slowly recovering his breath and strength. His body felt battered, bone tired and bruised, but he was alive. *I must be a witch,* he thought, managing a weak laugh at his miraculous survival. Then his thoughts immediately turned to Amber.

He spun around in the murky water, looking for her. The torrent had by now calmed into a wide river bounded by steep banks of red earth, green bushes and tall trees. But there was no sign of her in the water or along the banks. Connor began to despair. He'd failed to protect Henri and now Amber. He knew his snap decision to jump off the ledge had been risky. However, faced with certain death at the hands of the rebels or a slim chance of survival in the waterfall, he'd chosen the latter.

And now he was paying for that decision—with Amber's life.

Wearily, he began to swim for the bank. Then out of the corner of his eye he caught a glimpse of red hair trailing in the water and spotted an inert body floating downstream from him.

"Amber!" he shouted, paddling frantically in her direction.

There was no response. He kept going, despite the gnawing exhaustion in his limbs. Seeing a log drifting along with the current, a dozen or so feet ahead of him, he thought about using it for a float. Then the log swished its long scaly tail, propelling itself toward Amber's body. With primal horror Connor realized it was a crocodile.

"Amber!" he screamed as another croc slid from the bank into the river's murky waters.

She weakly lifted her head, smiling when she saw Connor waving at her.

"Crocodile!" he cried in warning.

Her smile evaporated as soon as she spotted the ominous snout and pair of slit-eyes gliding toward her. With furious strokes, she made for the bank. But the crocodile was closing in fast.

Connor swam for all he was worth. His daily pool training with Charley, which he'd begun in preparation for his previous assignment, was once again paying off as he cut through the water like a fish. He dug deep, calling upon hidden reserves of energy.

Amber was nearing the bank when the crocodile shot forward with a final burst of speed. Connor plunged on, determined to protect her, however impossible the odds.

Focused on its immediate prey, the crocodile didn't notice Connor's approach from upstream. As it opened its jaws to sink its teeth into Amber's trailing legs, Connor dived forward and wrapped his arms around the crocodile's snout. Praying Gunner was right about the weakness of their opening jaw muscles, Connor clung on with all his might, his legs wrapped around its body.

Unfamiliar with being the victim of an attack itself, the crocodile momentarily froze, and Connor found himself eye to eye with the prehistoric beast. It studied him with cold carnivorous intent. Then the crocodile wrenched its head away, its unimaginable brute strength trawling Connor through the water as it attempted to shake him off. But Connor refused to let go—he had to give Amber enough time to escape the river.

Besides, once he released the crocodile, *he* would become the prey.

Enraged, the crocodile dived beneath the surface. Connor barely managed to snatch a breath before he was dragged under with it. The crocodile rolled him, its tail whipping, its body writhing. Connor lost all sense of orientation. His arms became numb as he clung on for dear life. But it was no use. He was weakening with every passing second, and his lungs screamed for air. Forced to let go, Connor kicked himself away from the crocodile's jaws and came up gasping.

The crocodile vanished.

"Where's it gone?" he yelled, looking wildly around him.

Amber, who'd managed to crawl up onto the safety of the bank, scanned the river. Then she spotted a ripple on the surface moving toward him at high speed. "There!" she cried.

The water being shallow enough for him to touch the muddy riverbed, Connor half swam, half ran for the bank. He was waist-deep when the crocodile burst out of the water, its ferocious jaws open wide. It clamped down hard on Connor's back.

"*NO! Connor!*" Amber screamed as he was dragged back into the river and disappeared beneath the surface.

20

Water engulfed him once more, and Connor felt himself being tugged deeper and deeper. The sunlight faded to a murky twilight, and all sounds became a dull wash in his ears. Having seized its prey, the crocodile intended to drown him before devouring him. But its teeth had failed to sink into Connor's flesh. Instead all it had managed to gain was a mouthful of his go-bag.

Connor fought to free himself, but the straps were being pulled taut around his shoulders. He was entangled like a fish in a net. The crocodile settled on the riverbed and waited it out.

With every passing second, the urge to open his mouth and take a breath increased for Connor. The compulsion built like a wave until it threatened to overpower him. Connor judged he had less than a minute before his willpower gave out and his body's natural yet fatal reflexes took over.

At least his sacrifice meant something. He'd protected

his Principal with his life. No bodyguard could be asked to do more. He could only hope that Amber would reach the safety of the lodge on her own before any rebels caught up with her.

Connor continued to struggle, but his actions were becoming weaker and weaker. After all the ordeals he'd faced since the ambush, he had nothing left to give. His limbs were growing heavier, darkness was starting to encroach on his vision and he began to feel light-headed . . .

Out of the gloomy waters floated a ghostly apparition of his gran's face, stern but loving. *I want you to quit. Before something terrible happens to you.*

Sorry, Gran, he thought wistfully. *Too late.*

Her face faded, even as it mouthed the words in reply: *At what cost?*

Then a brighter vision appeared. Charley's angelic features, her long blond hair shimmering like a mermaid's. He heard himself say, *Yeah, but I'll survive.*

We're counting on it, Charley's vision replied. *Listen, I have to go. Stay safe.*

Connor didn't want her to go; he felt at peace with her. But he had no strength to call her back. All around him was now dark and cold. His mother's face swam into view. Not the lined, pained face he'd said farewell to after his birthday visit but the younger, happier one of his youth. The one he remembered before his mother had gotten her diagnosis of multiple sclerosis. She smiled at him. A sad smile of good-bye. Connor's heart ached as she too faded and another vision took its place.

His father.

Clearer than ever before, the rugged handsome features were like a well-worn map, his green-blue eyes shining with warmth in the darkness.

Connor grinned, his heart overwhelmed with joy at seeing him again.

But his father's expression remained firm as he whispered a familiar piece of fatherly advice: *Never give in. Never give up.*

But I want to be with you, thought Connor.

Don't you dare give up, son. It's not in our nature.

As his body's reflexes forced his mouth open and water entered, Connor's hand brushed against his father's knife on his hip. Like an electric spark, it revived him—a sliver of hope that spurred one final bid for survival.

Drawing the knife from its sheath with a hand tingling from numbness, Connor twisted his arm around and jabbed the blade's tip deep into the open eye of the crocodile. A dark red cloud of blood burst forth, and the animal immediately released its viselike grip on his back. Half blind and in agonizing pain, the crocodile jerked away and vanished into the murky depths of the river.

Fighting against his body's lead-like heaviness, Connor kicked for the surface. His head emerged and he gulped at the air, coughing and spluttering up the mouthful of water he'd swallowed. The hit of fresh oxygen to his lungs revived his senses, and with wild, desperate strokes he swam for the bank.

Bedraggled and half dead, he crawled through the muddy shallows. Amber rushed over and helped him stagger up the steep bank, away from the reach of any crocodiles. But they managed little more than twenty steps before they collapsed together beneath the protective shade of an acacia tree.

21

Yellow-breasted weaverbirds chirped merrily above the two prone bodies as they flitted in and out of their intricately woven nests, which adorned the tree's branches like dried fruit. A herd of tawny-colored impala, the males proudly displaying their long lyre-shaped horns, leisurely strolled past, heading toward the grassy plain to graze. And hippos wallowed in the cool, calm waters of the river, occasionally snorting or calling out in a series of deep lazy laughs. With the bright sunshine gilding the savannah, the scene couldn't have appeared more idyllic. Yet for the two broken individuals at the base of the tree, the paradise surrounding them was as dangerous and lethal as it was beautiful.

Connor had no idea how much time had passed since Amber had dragged him from the river's edge, but he had neither the strength nor the will to move again. He felt as if he'd gone ten rounds with a heavyweight boxer and been knocked out at every ring of the bell. His clothes were caked in mud and torn in several places. He was covered in abrasions, and there wasn't a single part of his body that didn't either ache or cry out in pain.

"I thought . . . I'd lost you for good," said Amber weakly.

Connor managed a weary shake of the head. "You can't get rid of me that easily."

Amber pushed herself up from the ground and winced, clenching her teeth against the pain.

"Are you okay?" Connor croaked.

"I think I lost most of my skin escaping that waterfall," she replied, lifting her T-shirt to examine the extent of her injuries. "More to the point, how are *you*?"

"I'm alive. Does that count?"

Amber managed the thinnest of laughs. "You're crazy, do you know that? Fighting crocodiles and leaping off waterfalls. Next time we climb down!"

"Fine by me," he replied, closing his eyes as a soft, warm breeze blew over them from the open savannah. At least they'd managed to cross the river. He listened to the gentle swishing of the long grasses, content not to move ever again.

Amber finished inspecting her wounds—the whole of her left side had been scraped red raw on the rocks, but nothing appeared to be broken—and then gasped as she caught sight of blood seeping into the earth.

"Connor, you're bleeding," she said, fighting to keep her voice steady.

Connor opened his eyes, the pain suddenly intensifying as he became conscious of his own injuries. Helping him sit up, Amber removed the tattered go-bag from his back and gingerly raised his shirt. Her sea-green eyes widened, and her mouth dropped open in shock.

"How bad is it?" asked Connor, terrified of what damage the crocodile had inflicted.

"There's barely a scratch on your back!" she remarked in astonishment. "A few nasty bruises. The bandage around your waist has come loose and the bullet wound's opened up again. But that's about it."

Connor breathed a painful sigh of relief. It was a miracle his spine hadn't been ripped out.

"I can't believe that crocodile didn't do more damage," Amber continued, tenderly touching his bare skin with her fingers. "I *saw* it bite into your back!"

A grin spread across Connor's face when he realized what had saved him from the animal's fearsome jaws. "The go-bag has a bulletproof body-armor panel built in," he explained. Then, with a laugh, he added, "I can't wait to see the look on Amir's face when I tell him the bag's croc-proof too!"

"Amir?" asked Amber.

"Yeah, one of my best friends at Guardian." Connor looked thoughtfully off toward the horizon. "I just hope he's faring better on his mission than I am."

"That wouldn't be hard," said Amber.

Connor's gaze dropped to the ground as a sharp stab of guilt and grief pierced his heart. "I'm sorry," he mumbled, unable to meet her eyes. "I'm so sorry. I promised to protect you and your brother, and I've failed."

Amber stared at him. "What are you talking about? You've done *everything* in your power to protect us. Who could have foreseen *any* of this happening? I only meant your friend couldn't be suffering as badly as you. It's not your fault that gunman killed my little brother . . . and my parents . . . It's *his!*"

Trembling with fury and deep loss, Amber lapsed into mournful silence. Connor reached over and took her hand, trying to offer her some comfort, conscious that words would have little effect. He knew from bitter experience the emotional devastation of losing a parent. But to have one's whole family torn from you in a matter of hours was something beyond grief. No words could ever describe the desolation experienced after such a loss.

Amber held his hand tight, almost squeezing the life from it. Then, eventually, her grip eased and she glanced down at his weeping wound.

"We need to take care of that," she said in a voice drained of all emotion.

Amber picked up the ravaged go-bag, but they didn't need to open it to see that most of the contents were missing. A huge hole had been ripped in the side. The binoculars were gone. So too was the water bottle, LifeStraw, sunblock and Maglite. Yet by some small grace of good fortune, the first-aid kit was still in its pouch. The case had been mauled to pieces, but Amber managed to cobble together enough to re-dress the wound and clean up his multitude of cuts. Then Connor tended to her injuries, Amber wincing as he gently pressed the last of the antiseptic wipes against her grazed skin. The cut on her lip was already healing, but the one on her cheek needed a fresh Band-Aid. As he applied it, their eyes met and he saw that hers were brimming over with tears.

"I loved my brother . . . you know," she confessed, choking back a sob. "He could be annoying at times . . . but what brother isn't? I just never told him . . . and now . . . I'll never get the chance."

22

Connor and Amber trudged through the brush in silence, heading south once more. Flies buzzed incessantly around them and the sun beat down, its punishing heat unrelenting. They heard gunshots somewhere in the distance, impelling them onward. As they dragged their feet through the long grass, hunger sapping at their strength with every step, their thirst intensified. But without the LifeStraw they didn't dare drink untreated water from the river, afraid not just of crocodiles but of getting sick.

The only items Connor now possessed were his Rangeman watch—still unblemished; his night-vision sunglasses—a little bent and scratched but serviceable; and his father's knife. He'd cut away the excess fabric of the go-bag, leaving the body-armor panel with its straps as a wearable shield in case they encountered the gunmen again.

Everything else had been lost—even hope.

But, spurred on by his father's words, Connor had eventually willed his battered body to rise and begin the long trek across the burning-hot savannah. As he put one weary foot in front of the other, his father's advice became a mantra in his head—*never give in, never give up, never give in, never give up* . . .

If they could only reach the lodge, their ordeal would be over. *For me, at least,* thought Connor as he glanced back at Amber.

Her head bowed and her hair hanging like a veil across her tearstained face, Amber's spirit was all but broken. Only Connor's dogged insistence that they keep going, that they not let the gunmen catch them or become carrion for the vultures, impelled her to move. But she was like a zombie, her eyes unfocused, back stooped and arms hanging loose, just shuffling along near the point of collapse.

Connor knew he looked equally battered. Their fraught escape through jungle, bush and river had taken its toll. With his tattered muddy clothes, innumerable cuts and scrapes, and half-loping gait caused by the painful gash in his side, he would be barely recognizable to his friends in Alpha team. However, the promise of water, food and medical assistance at the lodge kept his spirits up.

Emerging from the brush into a clearing, Connor checked the bearing on his compass watch to ensure they were still on track. As he looked up to gauge their next landmark, he found himself face-to-face with a buffalo.

The solitary bull glared at them from the other side of the clearing. The size of a small car and built like a tank, the buffalo was terrifying in its sheer barrel-shaped bulk, the massive curved horns almost three feet across. Flies scattered in a buzzing black cloud as the bull snorted angrily and shook its colossal head.

Drawing Amber closer to him, Connor took a cautious step back. Confronted by one of the most unpredictable and dangerous animals in Africa, they couldn't afford to provoke it in any way.

The old bull stamped a hoof, kicking up dust. Then, before they could retreat any farther, it released another explosive snort, lowered its head and charged.

Connor stood his ground, shielding Amber behind him. He simply didn't have the energy to run. And there were no trees close enough for them to climb out of danger anyway. His only defense was to show no fear in the face of the oncoming bull and pray it was a mock charge.

But the buffalo continued to thunder toward them like a runaway truck, its nostrils flaring, its battering ram of hardened bone targeted on Connor. They'd done nothing to antagonize the animal. But the beast seemed incensed.

Amber clung to him, too afraid to flee and too traumatized to cry out.

Connor squeezed his eyes shut as the bull bore down on them. He could hear the pounding hooves churning up the dirt and tensed in expectation of the bone-crushing impact. He tried not to imagine the crippling pain of being tossed high in the air, a bag of broken bones, or being gored by one of its horns and trampled to death.

His last act as bodyguard was to shove Amber aside.

Then a gunshot rang out, followed by two more in quick succession.

The buffalo was stopped in its tracks and Connor heard a heavy *whomp* as its mighty body hit the earth. On opening his eyes he was enveloped in a cloud of red dust. As the dust settled, the bull's head appeared inches from Connor's feet, blood streaming from several bullet holes on its neck, shoulder and flank. Its tongue lolled out and its eyes glazed over as the beast let out one final snort and succumbed to death.

Connor barely had time to register this when a voice with a slight Germanic accent barked, "What the heck are you two kids doing out here alone?"

From a dense thicket strode a white man in an olive-green shirt and knee-length shorts. Stocky, with a severe crew cut and gray-tinged beard, he was reloading a high-caliber bolt-action rifle fitted with a telescopic sight. In his wake trailed a thin black man wearing an earth-brown T-shirt and army surplus pants, shouldering a canvas pack.

Connor helped Amber to her feet. "Are you all right?" he asked.

Amber nodded.

"You could have been killed!" snapped the white man, inspecting the floored buffalo. Satisfied it was dead, he looked them up and down in wonder and horror. "My God, what happened to you?"

Judging by the man's attitude and appearance, he wasn't one of the rebels, and Connor felt safe enough to lower his guard and explain: "Our safari convoy"—he coughed, his throat dry and hoarse with dust—"was ambushed by gunmen yesterday."

"What gunmen are these?" asked the white man, offering Connor a hip flask of water.

Connor gulped down several mouthfuls before passing the flask to Amber to have the lion's share. The water revived him and he felt some of his strength return. "Rebel soldiers. Boys too. Possibly they're the ANL, led by a man known as the Black Mamba."

Both men's faces darkened at the mention of the rebel leader's name.

"We've been on the run ever since," Connor continued. "My friend here is the daughter of the French diplomat on an official goodwill visit to the park. We believe her parents, along with President Bagaza, have been murdered. So too has her little brother. We need to contact the authorities immediately."

With a pitying look at Amber, the white man nodded gravely. "This is serious."

He said some words to his companion in a language Connor didn't understand but presumed was the local dialect of Kirundi. The black man nodded and hurried off into the bush.

"You're lucky you ran into us," said the white man, turning back to them. "Listen, our camp isn't far from here. Come with me. We'll get you fed, watered and patched up. Then we'll sort this out."

Both Connor and Amber almost collapsed with relief.

Against all the odds, they'd been saved.

23

"My name is Jonas Wolff," said the white man as he escorted them through the bush. "But my friends call me the Wolf."

"Thank you for rescuing us, Wolf," said Amber.

"It was either that or watching you get trampled to death by a buffalo," he replied, his tone matter-of-fact and devoid of humor. "Those animals show no pity. They kill more people in Africa than any other large game."

"I was told hippos were the most dangerous."

The Wolf snorted dismissively. "The locals don't call a bull buffalo the Black Death for nothing. And such beasts don't go down easily. You're extremely fortunate that I'm a skilled marksman."

As they walked, the Wolf's eyes constantly scanned the savannah and he kept his rifle primed at all times. Connor was impressed by the man's vigilance. He was taking the threat of the rebels seriously.

At the foot of a hill they entered a large copse of trees,

pushing through the dense undergrowth until at its heart they came across a small rudimentary camp. Three green canvases were strung between the tree trunks, the make-shift shelters pitched around a fire in the center of a patch of cleared ground. To one side was a large pile of supplies, partly covered by a canvas, plus several jerry cans of water. Four men, including the one the Wolf had sent on ahead, eyed their arrival with curiosity as they squatted beside the fire, where a pot sat amid the glowing embers, its contents steaming.

"First, food and water," said the Wolf, gesturing for Amber and Connor to take a seat on a felled log next to the fire. "Abel, serve our guests."

As Connor and Amber settled down, grateful to rest their weary feet at last, the man in the army surplus pants lifted the pot's lid and gave the contents a stir, sending up a mouth-watering waft of braised meat. Abel passed them two tin plates piled high with a thick brown stew. Too hungry to mutter anything more than a quick thanks, Connor and Amber greedily tucked in.

"What is this?" asked Connor after polishing off his plate and receiving another helping. "It's delicious."

"Oryx," replied the Wolf, offering them both a brimming mug of water each.

Connor hadn't heard of the animal, but after eating snake, anything was a treat. He downed the water, ignoring its chlorinated taste, and the Wolf refilled his cup. As Connor drained that too, the Wolf noticed the bloodstain on his left side.

"Let me have a look at that," he said.

Connor took off his shirt, grimacing as pain flared through him.

The Wolf peeled back the bandage. "Nasty," he commented. "That'll need a few stitches."

Connor managed a wry smile. "I'm afraid I haven't come across any hospitals in this park yet."

"Not to worry. I can patch you up." The Wolf went over to the pile of supplies and returned with a medical kit. He took out an emergency suture pack. Removing Connor's bandage, he cleaned up the wound with a sterile saline solution, then laid out a scalpel, needle and thread.

"You've done this before?" asked Connor, growing more and more anxious as he watched the Wolf insert the thin nylon thread through the eye of the needle.

The Wolf nodded. "A few times. I trust you're not squeamish?"

Biting down on his lip, Connor winced as the Wolf cut away a small piece of loose flesh with the scalpel. Once satisfied the gash was even enough, he pinched the skin together to seal the wound. Then Connor felt the harsh sting of the needle's tip piercing his flesh, followed by a sharp tug as the Wolf tied off the first stitch. The process was repeated three more times, each stitch more agonizing than the last.

"All done," said the Wolf, cleaning away the blood with an antiseptic wipe.

A sheen of pained sweat on his brow, Connor glanced hesitantly down. The gash was as neatly sewn together as a woven shoelace.

"He's done a great job," said Amber encouragingly. She turned to the Wolf, who was packing away his suture kit. "Are you a doctor?"

"No. But I've had enough practice on myself," he explained, lifting his shirt to reveal a massive outline of scar tissue running across his chest and belly.

"What happened?" gasped Amber.

"A lion is what happened," he replied, but said no more. Re-dressing the stitched wound, the Wolf handed Connor two small foil packs. "Take these."

"What are they?" Connor asked.

"The white pills are painkillers."

Connor stared at him. "Couldn't you have given me these *before* you stitched me up?"

The Wolf shrugged indifferently. "They wouldn't have taken effect in time. The red-and-white ones are antibiotics. You'll need those to stop any infection. Take one a day for a week."

"Thanks," said Connor, immediately popping an antibiotic

and chasing it with a couple of painkillers. He slipped the remaining pills into his pocket.

"I don't know how we can ever repay you for your kindness," said Amber, setting aside her plate.

"In the bush, strangers are welcomed as family. You simply never know when *you* might need help." The Wolf stood and returned the medical kit to its place in the supply pile.

"So what are you and your men doing in the park?" asked Connor, putting his shirt back on. Revitalized by the meal, his senses were returning, and he noted that none of the group wore park ranger uniforms.

"We're conservationists," replied the Wolf. "Now, if you'll excuse me, I have to go back and examine that buffalo."

"But what about contacting the authorities?"

"That's all in hand," assured the Wolf, picking up his rifle. "Abel has put a call in on the radio. The best thing you two can do now is get some rest."

24

With food in their bellies, Connor and Amber were soon overcome by tiredness, and it didn't take much to persuade them to lie down beneath one of the canvases. Abel had laid out two bedrolls for them, and before their heads even hit the padded blankets, they were asleep.

Connor entered such a deep slumber that he struggled to rouse himself when he heard Amber arguing with someone.

"But I need to use the toilet," insisted Amber.

"Stay!" the man was saying.

Connor rose up on his elbows and saw Amber at the edge of the camp, attempting to get past one of the Wolf's men, a loose-limbed individual with tight-knit hair and bulging muscles that told of a hard life rather than days in the gym.

"Toilet," she repeated. "I have to go."

Immovable as stone, the man stared blankly at her.

"*Les toilettes,*" Amber repeated in French.

Comprehension lit up the man's face and he grunted, pointing to a tree a few yards away from the camp. Amber hurried toward it, disappearing into the undergrowth. But the man followed part of the way, keeping a close eye on her.

"*Arrêtez!*" he called after her. "*Pas plus loin.*"

Connor sat up and rubbed his eyes. The sleep had done him a world of good, and his strength had somewhat returned. His side still ached, though the pills had dulled some of the pain. Glancing at his watch, he saw it was past five o'clock in the afternoon. They'd been asleep for more than four hours. Connor took another dose of painkillers, then looked around the camp for the Wolf but couldn't see him. *Surely a rescue party from the lodge should have reached us by now.*

Stepping out from under the canvas, Connor felt the call of nature himself and headed into the bush. But Abel appeared in front of him, blocking his path.

"Where you go?" he asked.

"Toilet," replied Connor, then added for clarity, "*Les toilettes.*"

Abel moved aside. "Don't go far. Lions."

Connor nodded and walked a few yards away from the camp. As he relieved himself against a tree, he glanced back over his shoulder. Abel was watching him closely, and an uneasy feeling crept over Connor. Something was wrong here. Although he was only too aware of the dangers of the African bush and wouldn't have been surprised if there *had* been lions nearby, he was beginning to feel more like a prisoner than a guest.

When he returned to the camp, Amber was sitting by the fire, her expression unreadable.

Connor sat down next to her. "Are you okay?" he asked.

She nodded and smiled. But the smile seemed forced, more for the benefit of Abel and the muscleman still guarding the camp. Connor wondered where the Wolf and the other two men were. *Perhaps they've gone to meet the rescue party?* It seemed logical. After all, the Wolf had been nothing but hospitable toward them.

So why was his sixth sense for danger twitching?

Abel poured them some tea from a beaten-up kettle and handed them a packet of dry crackers each. Then he strolled over to his muscular friend and the two chatted in hushed tones to each other, every so often glancing in Connor and Amber's direction. The two men seemed on edge. But Connor reasoned that perhaps he was overreacting. Now that he'd told them about the Black Mamba and the rebel soldiers, they were probably concerned for their own lives.

Amber rested her head affectionately on his shoulder. Connor didn't mind but found it strange that she was being so familiar with him, considering their circumstances. Then she whispered in his ear, "I need to tell you something."

Connor nodded imperceptibly so as not to attract the attention of Abel or the other man.

"I spotted some camouflage netting when I went to the toilet. There were *six* elephant tusks hidden beneath it."

Connor immediately grasped the dangerous situation that put them in.

"The Wolf's no conservationist. He's a poacher," said Amber under her breath.

It all made perfect sense now. The hidden camp. The pile of supplies. The high-powered telescopic rifle. Even the enraged buffalo. Connor recalled seeing quite a few bullet holes in the slain animal. At the time of the attack he'd heard only three shots, but there had been some gunfire earlier in the distance. That suggested the bull was already injured and hurting when they came across it. Shot no doubt by the Wolf.

25

Before making any rash decisions, Connor needed to confirm his suspicions about their predicament. Leaving Amber by the fire, he strolled over to Abel and his friend where they squatted at the boundary of the camp. They stood at his approach, Abel's eyes narrowing and the muscleman crossing his arms.

"Where's the Wolf?" asked Connor nonchalantly.

"On a bushwalk," Abel replied.

"When will he be back?"

"Later."

"What about the authorities? When will they be arriving?"

"Soon."

Gathering he'd get little more than one-word answers from Abel, Connor tried a different tack.

"Can I use your radio, please?" he asked.

Abel shook his head.

"But I need to contact the lodge to—"

"No radio," he cut in.

"But Wolf said you—"

"He has the only radio."

Connor realized he was being stonewalled. He wouldn't find out anything further from Abel or his tight-lipped companion. However, he had all the answers he needed. The Wolf had said Abel had put a call in to the authorities. But how could he if the Wolf had the *only* radio?

He returned to sit beside Amber. Finishing his crackers, he said under his breath, "We need to leave."

"Surely we're safer here with the Wolf and his men than we'll be out there alone," Amber said, glancing nervously toward the savannah beyond the trees.

"Possibly," Connor replied. "However, I believe we're being held against our will. And I don't think they've called anyone for help."

"But the Wolf said—"

"I know what he said, but I'm certain he's lying. Which means no one knows where we are, or even that we're still alive."

Amber shook her head in disbelief. "Why would he lie to us?"

Connor looked at Amber. "He's an *illegal* poacher. He has no interest in contacting the authorities. So we have to leave while we can."

"Shouldn't we wait until morning at least?"

"Who knows what they've got planned for us? Besides, every hour that passes reduces our chances of getting out of here alive. The rebels will soon have control of the park, and with the president likely dead, they'll try to take over the country. That means civil war."

Amber nodded in reluctant agreement to his plan. Connor squeezed her hand reassuringly, then stood up to attract Abel's attention.

"We're going for a rest," he said, yawning and putting his hands together in a mime of sleep. By now the sun was low on the horizon, sending golden shafts of light through the copse's canopy. In less than an hour it would be dark.

Abel nodded, but kept his eye on them as they made their way over to the canvas shelter. Settling down on the bedrolls, Connor and Amber feigned sleep. Convinced by their act, Abel and Muscleman returned to their conversation. A short while later Connor heard them engrossed in a game of *igisoro*, having dug pits in the earth to make a temporary playing board. Connor nudged Amber, and as quietly as they could, they slid out of the back of the shelter and into the undergrowth. Ideally he'd have liked to take some supplies from the camp—at the very least a bottle of water—but he didn't want to risk arousing the men's suspicions. As soon as they were hidden from view, Connor crept with Amber between the trees toward the open savannah.

"Where do you think you're going?" growled a voice.

Connor and Amber stopped in their tracks as the Wolf materialized in front of them, his rifle unslung. The two other men from the camp stood behind him, menacing in their silence.

"To the safari lodge," said Connor, his tone defiant.

The Wolf glanced at the horizon, where the sun was beginning to settle. "Too dangerous. Dusk is prime hunting time for lions and hyenas."

"We're going anyway," Connor insisted, despite a frisson of fear running through his veins at the mention of hyenas.

"Not a wise decision. We spotted your rebels patrolling the plain."

"Better the devil we know," replied Amber.

The Wolf frowned. "What do you mean by that?"

"You haven't contacted the authorities, have you?" she accused.

The Wolf's face remained impassive, but there was a flicker of hesitation in his slate-gray eyes. "We've tried to get through, but no one's answering."

"We don't believe you," said Amber, her temper rising. "You're no conservationist! I've seen your stash of ivory. Now let us through."

She started to stride past, Connor keeping close by her side, but one of the men blocked their path, a bloodied machete hanging loose in his hand, the message chillingly clear.

The Wolf let out a heavy sigh and shook his head regretfully. "If you've seen the ivory, then I'm afraid I *definitely* can't let you go."

"We won't tell anyone about it," Connor assured him. "Or about you."

"I can't take that risk," he replied with an apologetic yet cold smile. "That ivory's worth over two million dollars on the black market. If the authorities are brought in, I stand to lose it all, including my freedom. So I'm sure you'll understand why you must stay in the camp. At least until the ivory's been transported out of the park."

Amber glared at the Wolf. "I thought you were a good man," she said bitterly. "But you're no better than those rebels out there. Killing innocent animals merely to line your own pockets. You're just a low-life *poacher!*"

The Wolf stared down his broad nose at her, offended to the core. "*I'm* one of the last great game hunters," he corrected her, his chest puffing up self-importantly. "Here in Africa to face down the Big Five."

With a grand sweep of his arm, he stepped aside to reveal the severed head of the bull buffalo lying in the grass. Its dead eyes stared blankly up at them, all its majestic might extinguished.

Proudly patting the buffalo's highly prized bossed horns, the Wolf declared, "Once I've completed my Big Five collection, I promise to deliver you to the authorities, safe and sound."

"And when might that be?" asked Connor.

"I've one more trophy to hunt down," the Wolf said, grinning. "The elusive leopard."

26

Connor and Amber were forced to sit by the fire as their hands and feet were bound.

"I regret having to do this," said the Wolf, watching Abel and the muscleman secure the wrist ties behind their backs, "but it's for your own good. The African bush is dangerous at night, and I can't have you wandering off."

"Please let us go," begged Amber.

"It's your own fault for prying, young lady," the Wolf snapped.

"But it could be days before you even find a leopard," Connor protested. "And rebel soldiers are swarming all over the park, you said so yourself. What if they find us first?"

The Wolf dismissed the suggestion with a snort of laughter. "The bush is my hunting ground. I can easily avoid those gung-ho rebels."

"But don't you understand what's happening here? They've killed or, at the very least, captured the president.

There's been a coup! This country is plunging into civil war. No one will be safe."

A smirk creasing his thin lips, the Wolf was apparently unfazed. "That all plays to my advantage. War brings chaos. There'll be no pesky rangers to protect the park, which makes it easier to smuggle out the ivory, along with my glorious collection."

Pulling back a canvas behind the pile of supplies, the Wolf unveiled a macabre row of animal heads and skins: a once-mighty lion with a full mane; a horned black rhino, its dark eyes weeping as if shedding tears; even a gargantuan elephant head with magnificent tusks; and to this sad line his men added the disembodied buffalo.

"You're a sick, sick man," said Amber, having to look away in sorrow and disgust.

The Wolf's eyes flashed with anger. "You know nothing, young lady. I'm preserving these animals forever. That's *true* conservation. We'll be able to admire these great beasts for years to come—"

"Can't you simply shoot them with a camera instead?" retorted Amber.

The Wolf's brow knitted in bewilderment. "Where's the thrill in that? I'm hunting these animals on foot. My life is on the line just as much as theirs. That's what makes it—" The Wolf stopped talking as a repeated growl, like wood being sawed, was heard amid the early-evening chorus of the savannah.

His eyes lit up. *"Leopard!"* he gasped.

Snatching up his rifle, he barked orders to his men, grabbed a handful of spare cartridges and refilled his hip flask from a jerry can. Abel shouldered the kit bag and they prepared to leave. At the edge of the camp, the Wolf glanced back over his shoulder at Connor and Amber on the ground, almost seeming to have forgotten them in his excitement.

"Don't try to escape!" he warned, his eyes narrowing. "Otherwise I'll hunt *you* down for my collection too."

Accompanied by Abel, he trekked off into the darkening twilight.

Amber glared at his receding shadow. "I wish that lion had eaten him!"

Connor nodded his agreement.

Muscleman and the two others remained behind at the camp, ostensibly to guard them. But, bound as they were, they were paid little attention by the men, who soon became involved in another game of *igisoro*. As dusk fell, the poachers rebuilt the fire and reheated the oryx stew. They didn't share their meal this time, although one of them, the youngest, made sure their captives each drank a mugful of water. Then, squatting on the opposite side of the fire, the three men chatted to one another in hushed tones, occasionally glancing over at Connor and Amber propped up against the log in the darkness.

"Can you understand anything they're saying?" Connor whispered, wishing he had his smartphone to translate.

Shifting closer, Amber replied softly, "They're talking about what to do with us."

The look of horror and dismay in her eyes didn't fill Connor with optimism.

"Muscleman wants to feed us to the lions," she explained. "The one with the mustache wants to hand us over to the rebels in return for safe passage. And the younger poacher thinks they should just leave us here when they go."

"None of those options sound particularly promising," Connor remarked, "or what the Wolf threatened us with."

Firelight flickering across her face, Amber offered him a resigned smile. "They're also talking about the return of the Black Mamba. They sound pretty scared, even Musclema—"

"*Tais-toi!*" snapped Muscleman, ordering them to be quiet.

As they sat in enforced silence, the ache in their wrists and ankles growing steadily worse because of the tight bindings, Connor considered the implications of what Amber had just told him. It seemed as if they'd jumped out of the frying pan and into the fire—fleeing the rebels only to become prisoners of the poachers, a death sentence almost certainly hanging over their heads.

27

It was late when the poachers finally settled down beneath their makeshift tents, leaving the younger one beside the fire to watch over their prisoners. Amber lay contorted on the hard earth, her body twisted awkwardly by the bindings as she tried to sleep. Connor, however, was in no state of mind to rest. Through half-closed eyes, he observed their guard absently chipping away at the log with his father's knife and tried to figure out how to free them both and get his heirloom back.

The Wolf and Abel had yet to return. With the other two asleep, Connor reckoned this was their best opportunity to attempt an escape. For, despite the Wolf's initial aid, Connor couldn't trust the man to stay true to his word. Even if it was the hunter's intention to release them to the authorities, his gang of poachers could well persuade him to do otherwise.

Their only chance of survival lay in running.

The sound of chipping wood ceased and Connor cautiously looked up. Their guard was beginning to doze, his head lolling, the knife left protruding out of the hacked piece of log. Connor waited another ten minutes, then, as quietly as he could, shifted into a kneeling position. It took some time, his limbs being stiff and his muscles cramped, but eventually he got himself upright. Although his hands were numb, the blood supply half cut off, Connor was glad his bindings were tight. It would make them easier to break.

Bending over, he raised his arms behind himself and, just as he'd been shown at his surprise birthday party, brought them down hard onto his backside. But the impact failed to snap the plastic tie. Instead he lost his balance, toppled forward and landed face-first in the dirt.

Spitting out bits of earth, Connor twisted his head around toward the guard. Thankfully the young poacher was still asleep. Convinced the technique had been easier in the company of his friends, Connor made sure the tie's locking mechanism was dead-center between his wrists and tried again. It took two more attempts before the binding actually split.

After shaking the blood back into his hands, he edged his way over to the sleeping guard and reached for his knife. The young man stirred, and Connor's fingers clasped the hilt of the knife, ready to fight back. But the poacher didn't wake, and Connor relaxed his grip. Tugging the blade free, he sliced through the plastic binding securing his ankles. Then he crept back to Amber and placed a finger on her lips.

Her eyes flickered open and she flinched away, but immediately calmed on seeing Connor's face in the firelight. Connor cut her ties, then signed for her to follow him. They passed the supply pile, where he grabbed a full water bottle and found his discarded go-bag. Leaving the muted glow of the campfire behind, the night closed in around them until they could barely see in front of their faces. From the pocket of his cargo pants Connor retrieved his night-vision sunglasses. Flicking the tiny switch on the frame's edge, the world burst back into a ghostly light. Almost immediately he was confronted by a pair of huge round eyes and almost cried out—but it was just a harmless bush baby hanging from a nearby branch.

With the copse now illuminated as if there was a full moon, Connor saw a track they could follow through the undergrowth without making a sound. But they'd only gone a few yards when Muscleman stepped out from behind a tree. Having just finished relieving himself, the poacher looked as surprised as they were. Before he could react, Connor drove a fist into the man's gut with a stepping lunge punch; it was like hitting a solid brick wall. For all his martial arts expertise, his fist crumpled against the granite-hard stomach.

Muscleman grinned in amusement, his teeth gleaming like a half-moon in the darkness.

"Encore!" He laughed, opening up his arms to welcome another shot.

In the second that Connor took to consider his next best target, Amber stepped up and kicked Muscleman straight between the legs. The poacher's eyes bulged and he bent double, expelling a pained gasp. Then she hammer-fisted him in the temple. Muscleman went down like a felled buffalo.

Connor stared at Amber in stunned admiration.

She replied with a shrug, "That's what they taught me to do in self-defense class at school."

"Then remind me never to pick a fight with you!"

28

Connor and Amber crept through a night alive with noise and unseen movement. The warm air pulsated with the ceaseless chirp of crickets and cicadas, the plaintive cries of bush babies and the soft flutter of bats flying overhead. Accompanying this nightly chorus of the African savannah were the rumbling vocalizations of elephants and the deep drawn-out roars of lions prowling the plain.

Connor's eyes darted to every snap of twig or rustle of leaf in the darkness. But even with the aid of his night-vision glasses, he rarely saw the culprit—the creature disappearing into the bushes or up into the branches before he could identify it.

Amber kept a firm grip on his hand, anxious not to lose him in the unnerving dark as he guided her through the trees bordering the plain. Every so often he'd check the compass on his watch and adjust their direction. Connor had made the conscious decision not to take the most direct route to the lodge, fearing that if they broke the cover of the trees, they'd be more easily spotted by rebel soldiers or the Wolf, or else become prey to the lions they could hear hunting.

Neither of them spoke as they hurried away from the camp. Connor presumed that Muscleman must have come to and woken the others by now. But would they come after them in the dark and without the Wolf?

Connor heard another crack of a twig close by.

He stopped still and Amber became motionless by his side. Her labored breathing was loud in his ear as he strained to listen for what animal or person was approaching. But the night noises gave nothing away.

Continuing on, they kept to a well-used animal trail. This made the going easier and quicker, as well as hiding any potential tracks they made among the spoor of antelope and other creatures. If the Wolf really did mean to hunt them down, Connor wanted to ensure he left as little evidence of their progress as possible.

Out of the corner of his eye, he caught a flash of movement.

Connor spun in its direction.

"What is it?" Amber whispered, her eyes wide as a bush baby's.

Connor shushed for her to be silent. He scanned the bushes, their edges glowing softly in his night vision. A branch was swaying ever so slightly, but there was nothing there.

"Just my imagination," he replied, keeping his voice low as he led Amber farther along the trail. But they hadn't gone far when they both heard a distinct rustling.

Was the Wolf on their trail already? Or had they run into a rebel patrol?

Connor slowly pivoted on the spot, searching the undergrowth once more. But it was just a shadowy wall of bushes and grass.

Then he happened to glance up.

Peering menacingly from the bough of a tree were two glassy green orbs.

Without his night vision the leopard would have been entirely invisible to him, a ghost in the night. But Connor could just about discern the sleek outline of the big cat, the white tip of its tail twitching . . . then a flash of its fearsome pointed canines as it opened its jaws and pounced from the tree.

29

"I'm getting nowhere," explained an infuriated Charley to Colonel Black in his office. "Connor's phone isn't responding. The safari lodge is no longer answering. The Burundian French embassy's closed for the weekend and their emergency number goes straight to voice mail. When I did eventually manage to reach President Bagaza's office in Bujumbura, the secretary said that she'd get back to me right away, but that was four hours ago and I still haven't heard anything from her. What's more, that office is about to close too."

"Typical!" said Colonel Black, his expression both sympathetic and grim. "Have you tried calling the hospitals?"

Charley nodded. "Only one answered, and I spoke to some poor overworked doctor, Dr. Emmanuel Ndayi . . . Ndayikunda, or at least I think that's how you pronounce it. He said he'd check the records for me now. I'm still waiting for his call back."

"Don't hold out too much hope," replied the colonel,

leaning forward and resting his elbows on the desk. "From my experience of Africa, 'now' means sometime in the next few days."

"So what *can* we do?" Charley implored, her hands gripping the armrests of her chair in frustration. "Connor's missed all his report-ins for the past twenty-four hours. Something's gone drastically wrong. I feel it in my heart."

"I agree. A communication blackout of this length warrants emergency action." The colonel picked up the phone. "Let's contact the Burundian commander in chief and see if he has any news of the situation."

Colonel Black dialed a number that took him straight through to the military headquarters in Burundi. After speaking with several subordinates, he eventually worked his way up the ranks and was put through to the man himself.

"Major General Tabu Baratuza here," barked the commander in chief over the speakerphone. "How can I be of assistance, Colonel? But please be quick. I was due at a formal dinner an hour ago."

"My apologies for disturbing you this evening, General. However, we have a legitimate cause for concern regarding the well-being of your president and the visiting French diplomat and his family."

"Go on," said the major general, the softening of his tone indicating that the colonel had captured his full attention.

"We have a security operative protecting the French

diplomat's children," Colonel Black explained. "For the past twenty-four hours we've had no contact from him, and we can't reach the party by any other means. This is highly irregular. Have you had any recent communication with the president or his guard at the Ruvubu safari lodge?"

The major general paused a moment before replying, clearly evaluating his own answer. "Yes. I received a request from the president the other day to send some soldiers into sector eight of Ruvubu National Park."

"For what reason?"

"I'm not at liberty to divulge such information. But this morning that request was canceled."

Colonel Black frowned. "Isn't that rather unusual?"

"Not really. The president is known for changing his mind."

The colonel leaned back in his leather chair, a deeply pensive expression on his face. "Before we lost contact, our operative mentioned rumors of the Black Mamba. I am wondering if this is somehow connected to our operative's lack of comms."

The major general cleared his throat. "I've heard those rumors too. But I can assure you that they're just rumors. However, Colonel, I'll look into your concerns *now now* and ensure someone gets back to you. Have a good evening."

As the Burundian commander in chief cut the connection, Colonel Black raised a surprised eyebrow at Charley.

"He'll look into it *now now*! If we're lucky, that means we might hear back within an hour. Don't hold your breath, though."

But the colonel was proved wrong. They only had to wait half that time before the major general himself called them back.

"Colonel, we're getting zero response from the presidential guard or any of our soldiers stationed there," he informed them. "I hope it's just a comms issue, but to be sure, I'm dispatching a unit of troops to the park immediately. They'll be there at first light."

30

A spine-chilling growl. A slash of razor-sharp claws. A dead weight landing on his shoulders, knocking him to the ground. Amber pinned beneath him, screaming. Claws raking into his back. Snarling jaws ripping apart his go-bag. His vision filling with a blinding fire. Then blackness...

Connor parted his eyes. The early glow of dawn was visible on the horizon. Birds sang softly from the trees, and insects hummed in the long grass. The embers of a campfire smoldered gently, sending up a plume of hazy gray smoke. In the middle was a flat rock upon which three plump white sausages sizzled, browning as they cooked.

Lying prone on the ground, Connor felt as if his back was on fire, cooking like those sausages. Then someone pressed a smooth paste into his wounds, soothing the burning sensation. As the pain subsided, Connor sighed and closed his eyes. But the relief was short-lived. All of a sudden he felt a sharp pinch on his shoulder as if he'd been bitten.

Looking for the source of the attack, he saw a young black girl with rounded cheeks and bright eyes kneeling beside him. He also spotted four raw bloody lines across his left shoulder, scored by the claws of the leopard, one gouge particularly deep. The girl applied more red-brown paste to this cut, then held a wriggling driver ant between her fingertips and brought the insect near the wound.

"No!" he croaked, but he was too late to stop her.

The driver ant's pincers bit either side of his cut, closing the wound. As soon as its jaws had clamped on to his skin, the girl ripped the ant's body off, leaving the head behind. Too stunned and too weak to protest, Connor watched as she methodically stitched together his injury with live driver ants. Soon he had a neat row of ant heads, like black sequins, across his shoulder.

"Who are you?" he groaned when she'd finished.

"Her name's Zuzu," replied Amber on the girl's behalf. "She's from a nearby Batwa tribe."

Connor turned his aching head the other way. Amber was sitting on a rock, picking at the dry white flesh of a baobab fruit and chewing contentedly. "You saved my life yet again," she said.

"Did I?"

Amber smiled. "Don't you remember?"

Connor shook his head. For him the whole experience of the leopard attack was a fragmented series of flashing nightmares.

"All I heard was this terrifying roar," she explained. "I couldn't see a thing. But you wrapped yourself around me, shielding me from the leopard. You wouldn't let go, even though the leopard was ripping *you* to shreds." Amber shook her head in disbelief at his courageous act. "Now I know what you mean by body cover!"

She winked at him and took a sip from the water bottle stolen from the poacher's camp.

Connor tried to sit up, but pain flared across his back.

"Is it bad?" he asked, imagining his skin flayed and the flesh stripped to the bone.

Amber glanced at his wounds and grimaced. Then she asked Zuzu, *"Est-ce qu'il va s'en sortir?"*

The girl replied in French and Amber translated, "Zuzu says they have a saying in their tribe: *From every wound there is a scar. And every scar tells a story. A story that says, 'I survived.'* So I think that means you'll live."

Amber held up the tattered remains of his go-bag. "But I'm afraid your backpack isn't leopard-proof."

She then showed him his bloodstained shirt. Four claw marks were ripped across one shoulder, but the rest of the fabric was undamaged. "What saved you was your shirt! I've no idea how, but it's a miracle your back wasn't torn apart."

"The shirt's stab-proof," Connor explained, groaning as Zuzu helped him into a sitting position. "Unfortunately, it doesn't keep you from being beaten to a pulp. But how on earth did we escape the leopard?"

Amber directed her gaze to Zuzu. "That's thanks to our new friend here. Zuzu was camped nearby. She heard my screaming and came running. She chased off the leopard with a flaming branch from her fire."

Zuzu rattled off some more words as she lightly rubbed the oil from a split aloe-vera stem on Connor's bruises and scrapes, delivering instant relief. Connor looked to Amber for a translation.

"She says we're extremely lucky to have survived the attack. That particular leopard's known among her tribe as the Spotted Devil. It's a man-eater!"

As Amber told him this, there was an incongruous smile on her face.

"What are you looking so happy about?" asked Connor, perplexed by her upbeat mood. "We could have been killed!"

Her smile widened. "Henri's alive!"

31

Any pain Connor had been feeling was washed aside by a wave of elation. He couldn't believe what he was hearing. He'd given Henri up for dead.

"How do you know this? Where is he?" Connor asked hurriedly.

"Zuzu saw a group of rebel soldiers taking a white boy with red hair toward Dead Man's Hill," Amber explained as she passed him the water bottle. "It can only be my brother."

"We should have known that rebel was lying to us!" muttered Connor, shaking his head bitterly at the man's callous deceit. Taking a swig from the water bottle, he knocked back another antibiotic and a couple more painkillers. "We have to reach the lodge as soon as possible and—"

"No," cut in Amber. "We're going to Dead Man's Hill."

Connor blinked, stunned at her unexpected announcement. "But we don't even know where that is from here."

"Zuzu does. She says it's that way," responded Amber,

pointing north across the plain. "And she'll guide us there."

The bushgirl nodded emphatically as she finished tending to his back.

"But that's the opposite direction from the lodge," said Connor. "Besides, what are you planning to do when we get there?"

"Rescue my brother, of course."

Connor stared openmouthed at Amber, wondering if she'd lost her grip on reality. "Look, we're tired, hungry and hurting. We're in no state to launch a rescue mission. More to the point, those rebels won't let us simply stroll into their camp and take Henri from under their noses. Not without a fight."

"I know that," snapped Amber, glaring at him for even suggesting she was so naive. "But if we don't try to rescue him now, we might never find him again . . . alive, at least."

Connor rubbed his dirt-stained face between his hands and sighed wearily. "I realize you want to do everything you can to save your brother. I'm as desperate as you to get him back safe and sound. But I can't have you risking your life in a suicide mission. I honestly think our best plan is to return to the lodge and call for backup."

"And how long will that take? A day? Two days? Maybe more in this godforsaken country. We don't have that time to waste. Every minute counts. Who knows what they're doing to my brother? Henri's life could be in the balance."

"And so is yours," said Connor, torn between rescuing Henri and keeping Amber out of danger. His head told him one thing; his heart, the other. In the end, reason won out. "I'm sorry, but I can't let you go. It's too much of a risk."

Amber looked at him, her eyes blazing. "I lost Henri once. I won't lose him again. He's the only family I have left. I *have* to save my brother." She stabbed a finger at him. "*You* have to save my brother. You're supposed to be his bodyguard, aren't you?"

"I'm your bodyguard too," he reminded her. "I have a duty to keep you *both* safe from harm."

Amber stood and crossed her arms defiantly. "Well, then, you'll have to protect me rescuing him. Because I'm going, with or without you!"

32

"Your parents are dead!" Blaze shouted as he struck Henri with a long, thin bamboo cane. *Whack!*

Henri fell to the rocky ground, crying out in agonized shock as a large red welt flared across his upper arm.

"Your parents were weak. They failed to protect you." *Whack!*

Tears burst from Henri's eyes as the cane whipped across his back, the pain so intense that he couldn't even cry out.

"Your sister ran away." *Whack!*

Henri instinctively curled into the fetal position, his hands over his head, as more blows rained down.

"Did you hear me? She failed to protect you too."

Whack! Whack!

"Now she's dead. So is her boyfriend. And you're all alone."

No Mercy watched impassively as Blaze beat the white boy. He recalled his own initiation ritual beginning in a similar way. Having been abducted from his village, he was beaten day and night until his body and spirit were broken down to nothing. Poisonous words were whispered in his ear to convince him of his family's treachery and abandonment before their deaths at the hands of a rival rebel group. Then the Black Mamba had come to him, offering salvation and relief from the constant physical and mental abuse. At that point, lost in a world of pain and grief, he'd been willing to do anything to make the unbearable suffering stop. *Anything.* Even kill a man with his bare hands. That's when he was reborn, piece by piece, killing by killing. The Black Mamba rebuilt him into a warrior, a soldier of God. Gave him a new name. His past was no longer relevant. He existed purely to fight and die as if there were no tomorrow.

Blaze ceased his brutal punishment of the boy.

Wheezing and sobbing, Henri lay trembling on the rocks, a splatter of his blood smeared across their surface. Kneeling down, Blaze gently ran a hand through the boy's red hair.

"But we can protect you," he said softly in the boy's ear. "We can make you strong. But first you must prove yourself. Earn our respect. Become worthy of the name Red Devil."

The sound of an approaching jeep caused Blaze and No Mercy to look up.

General Pascal had returned from the lodge, bringing with him the Gray Man, as they now all called him.

"Put the boy to work with the others," ordered Blaze, handing No Mercy the bamboo cane. "And beat him if he slows or stops."

Nodding, No Mercy dragged Henri to his feet and half carried him over to where the enslaved workers were digging up and panning the riverbed. Blaze strode across the river to greet the general, saluting him as he stepped out of the jeep with the Gray Man.

"Welcome, Mr. Gray, to Diamond Valley," declared General Pascal with a majestic sweep of his arm at the hidden gorge being stripped back and plundered. "That's what I call it anyway. This place is so rich with minerals that at night the ground sparkles as if the stars had fallen from the sky."

"Very poetic," replied Mr. Gray flatly, without any real sign of appreciation. His almost colorless eyes were trained on No Mercy, handing a battered bucket to a bleeding and sobbing child. "Who's the white boy?" he asked.

"Some foreign diplomat's son." The general laughed as he waved his hand dismissively. "White men are always taking from our country. It's time for them to pay the price."

"You could ransom him," suggested Mr. Gray. "He'd have value."

"Why? I have all the riches I need here," retorted the general.

Ordering Blaze to bring over the lockbox from his tent, he opened the lid and spread out a collection of rough diamonds on the hood of the jeep. "Now let's do business, Mr. Gray. Take your pick. I want to have the best-equipped army in Africa."

33

Striking camp, Connor, Amber and Zuzu set forth across the plain. Zuzu walked ahead, her bare feet noiseless on the red earth. Her body small and slender like a gazelle's, she wore a mottled-brown wraparound sarong, with a simple shawl slung over her left shoulder. In her right hand she carried a wooden bow and several black-tipped arrows. Aside from a gourd containing water, a fire-lighting stick and a small knife, she possessed little else.

Connor was amazed that she could survive in such a wild place with no supplies. When he'd asked her about this through Amber, she'd replied that the land provided all she needed to live. And, as if to prove her point, she'd plucked some small orange berries from a nearby bush and popped them into her mouth before offering some to them. The fruits were bittersweet, but a great deal more palatable than the "sausage" Connor had consumed for their bush breakfast.

Earlier that morning, as he'd wrestled over the dilemma

of whether to let Amber attempt to rescue her brother, Zuzu had handed him one of the plump white blobs cooking on the open fire and he'd bitten into it with barely a second thought. He soon discovered that the "sausage" had a strange fluid consistency and tasted a bit like a nutty mushroom, but rather less pleasant. Zuzu had looked on encouragingly as he chewed. Then Amber had taken great pleasure in informing him that he was eating fried rhino-beetle larvae! He'd almost gagged but managed to keep the smile on his face for Zuzu's benefit, reminding himself that the larva was a bush delicacy. But rather than subject himself to a second helping, he'd hurriedly agreed to Amber's change of plan. Besides, he'd realized that he couldn't carry his Principal kicking and screaming all the way back to the lodge. Nor could he leave her to walk alone and unprotected into a kill zone. And, the most persuasive reason of all, how could he live with himself if, as his bodyguard, he abandoned Henri to his fate?

Yet as they followed Zuzu through the stiflingly hot bush, Connor began to question the wisdom of his decision. Lacking Zuzu's intimate knowledge of bushcraft and now possessing only his father's knife—the night-vision sunglasses having been crushed beyond repair during the leopard attack—he felt woefully underprepared for the ordeal ahead. It seemed as if they were about to enter the lion's den with little more than a toothpick for protection.

Moreover, he couldn't believe they were putting their lives into the hands of a complete stranger again. They'd done that once with the Wolf and almost paid the price.

Connor quietly drew up beside Amber. "Are you sure we can trust our guide?" he whispered, avoiding using Zuzu's name in case she realized he was talking about her.

"Why not?" said Amber, surprised by the question.

"For all we know, she could be leading us into a trap. Maybe hoping for payment from the rebels for finding us."

Amber frowned at Connor. "I can't believe *everyone* in this country is corrupt. She saved our lives, remember? In fact, she tried to dissuade me from going to Dead Man's Hill in the first place, saying it's cursed by evil spirits and is where that leopard lives."

"Now you tell me!" said Connor, feeling somewhat duped into agreeing to their crazy rescue mission.

Amber kept talking as if she hadn't heard him. "But I told her how much my brother meant to me and she understood, having lost a brother herself."

"Even so, we know nothing about her," Connor argued, keeping his voice low.

"I do," replied Amber. "While you were out cold, we talked a lot."

Zuzu glanced over her shoulder to make sure they were still keeping up. Her smile was bright and innocent, and Connor couldn't detect any trace of deception in her eyes.

He felt a touch guilty about talking behind her back, but it was a bodyguard's job to be suspicious—at least until the person in question proved worthy of trust. He'd learned that lesson with the Wolf.

"It's a really sad story," Amber explained. "Remember I told you that Zuzu's from one of the local Batwa tribes? Well, the government forced them out of their ancestral lands to create this national park. Minister Feruzi was lying when he said that the Batwa had been given lovely new homes, schools and freshwater wells. The tribes were lucky to get a well, let alone housing. Most were given no land and left to fend for themselves. Zuzu tells me only a few Batwa men were offered work in the park, despite their knowledge of the bush, so many have had to resort to begging or manual labor just to survive. Zuzu and her family are essentially conservation refugees."

"So how come she's in the park if it's a restricted area?" questioned Connor.

"Hunting for food," replied Amber. "The Batwa are traditionally hunter-gatherers. Since her father died—she said his heart was broken after losing both his son and his homeland—it's fallen to Zuzu to provide for the entire family. But the government's outlawed all forms of game-hunting. So if she's caught, she'll be arrested as a poacher, and then she doesn't know how they'll survi—"

Up ahead Zuzu suddenly became still as a rock, her hand

held up in warning for them to be silent. Connor's eyes immediately scanned their surroundings, searching for the threat. With infinite care Zuzu nocked an arrow and took aim at something hidden among the brush. Connor's hand went to his knife. The savannah around them grew deadly quiet, as if sensing the danger in their vicinity. Connor felt his pulse quicken and drew Amber closer, ready to protect her from whatever predator appeared.

All of a sudden Zuzu let loose her arrow and disappeared into the long grass. Connor only caught a glimpse of her lithe body as she silently dashed through the brush. Grabbing Amber's hand, he pursued their guide, not wanting to let her out of his sight. They caught up with her in a small clearing, kneeling beside a dying dik-dik.

It dawned on Connor that *Zuzu* had been the predator the savannah had gone silent for.

Plucking her arrow from the tiny antelope's chest and putting it aside, she laid her hands on the animal and softly uttered what sounded to Connor like a blessing. Then Zuzu glanced up and spoke to Amber.

"The Batwa take what they can, but only what they need," Amber translated for Connor.

As Zuzu bound the little antelope's hooves together, Connor went to help by picking up the discarded arrow. But Zuzu quickly said, *"Ne touchez pas! C'est toxique!"*

"Stop!" Amber warned. "The tip's poisonous."

Connor nodded, leaving the deadly arrow where it lay. "Yeah, I got the gist."

Zuzu slung the dead antelope over her shoulder. "*A manger,*" she said with a smile before picking up her bow and arrows and continuing along their previous trail.

Astounded at her expert hunting skills, Connor and Amber followed, speechless, in her wake. Zuzu's pace was steady yet relentless. She seemed neither to need rest nor to drink water, and despite the disorienting nature of the landscape, always appeared to know exactly where she was headed, following trails and tracks invisible to their eyes.

Having heard Zuzu's story, Connor felt a little reassured about their guide but still questioned her motive for helping them. If her family was that desperate, surely she'd be tempted to sell Amber and him to the rebels at the first opportunity. He resolved to keep a careful eye on her.

After two hours' solid trekking beneath the sweltering sun, he and Amber were beginning to flag. Just as he was about to ask Zuzu to stop, she pointed to a craggy peak in the distance, atop which perched a lone acacia tree: Dead Man's Hill.

34

Too late to turn back now, thought Connor, steeling himself for the climb ahead.

At the base of the hill, Zuzu halted for a water break and took a measured sip from her gourd. Severely dehydrated from their long trek, Connor and Amber sat down on a rock and drained their remaining supply in one swig. Connor held out the upturned bottle to Zuzu to indicate it was empty. She smiled, said something to him and pointed to the slope.

"There's a freshwater spring halfway up," interpreted Amber.

Guessing they might be hungry too, their guide strolled over to a clump of palm trees. With the accuracy of a sharp-shooter, she slung a rock up into its branches and knocked down three round red fruit. The shiny outer skin was as hard as a nut, but Zuzu showed them how to crack it open with a stick. Connor was taken aback at the flavor: the light brown flesh inside tasted just like dried ginger cake.

"It's as if she's walking around her very own supermarket!" remarked Amber, tucking into the unexpected treat.

Reenergized, Connor got back to his feet, ready to tackle the hill. However, Zuzu remained squatting on her haunches, picking at her fruit. "Aren't you coming?" he asked.

Zuzu shook her head, her eyes glancing fearfully up at the peak as she replied in French.

Amber translated, "She says she'll wait here until we return with Henri, then guide us back to the lodge."

Connor stared at Amber. "We can't go on without her," he said firmly. "We have no idea what's on the other side or where your brother might be." And, although he didn't say it, he had no intention of letting their guide out of his sight.

"But she's adamant she won't go," replied Amber.

"Then we're not going either. If we have to make a quick getaway, we'll need Zuzu's local knowledge."

"But . . ." Amber stopped. Connor's stern expression told her there'd be no negotiation on the point.

Kneeling down beside Zuzu, she spoke rapidly in French, her tone shifting from gentle cajoling to obvious pleading. Zuzu was distinctly reluctant, repeatedly mentioning *les specters* and *le léopard*. The conviction of her objections was making Connor ever more uneasy at the prospect of scaling Dead Man's Hill. Eventually, though, Zuzu caved in to Amber's pleas and nodded. As she rose to her feet and picked up her bow and arrow, Amber glanced over her shoulder at Connor with a triumphant yet strained smile.

"How did you persuade her?" he asked.

"I told her that you're a mighty warrior in your land and have the power to protect us from all evil."

"No pressure, then," said Connor.

"I also offered her the pick of my clothes and jewelry when we return to the lodge," Amber admitted.

Connor did a double take. "She's taking us up the hill for a *dress*?"

Amber nodded. "In part. That sarong and shawl are the only clothes she owns. Zuzu thought it more than a fair trade for her services as a guide. But in truth, I think she's doing it out of the goodness of her heart. Having lost her own brother, she understands my need to save Henri."

Zuzu led them through the scrub and up a winding animal trail. She climbed the rocky slope as surefooted as a mountain goat, making Connor feel distinctly unfit and ungainly by comparison. Even Amber was struggling, despite her climbing skills. Zuzu kept looking furtively around, but nothing hostile materialized. The ascent was hot, tiring work, and Connor was glad for the spring halfway up, where they could replenish their water bottle and cool down.

By the time they neared the peak, the sun had passed its zenith. The ancient acacia tree cast a dark shadow that looked like a twisted and tortured man upon the bare sun-bleached rock. As they approached, Zuzu slowed and became even more guarded in her tread. Clearly nervous, she indicated for them both to keep low and stay silent. Hiding behind a boulder, the three of them cautiously peered over the edge.

Connor was astounded at what he saw.

They had a bird's-eye view over the hidden valley. Protected by its steep sides and fed by a number of springs, a thick blanket of trees and plants had flourished in the natural haven. The lush foliage cascaded down like a green curtain to a broad glistening river below, which snaked its way toward a drop-off to feed the Ruvubu River in the distance. It was as if they were staring into a lost world, except for the fact that the landscape was being torn apart and the river had been dammed. At the bottom of the valley, bare-chested workers toiled with picks and shovels, ripping up the soil and clearing away the vegetation. Others were sifting through piles of dirt or panning the muddied waters with rusting metal sieves. Dotted around this scene of devastation like an army of soldier ants were boys toting AK-47s.

Zuzu sorrowfully shook her head at the sight. *"On dirait qu'ils mangent de la terre."*

Connor looked to Amber.

"She says, it looks like they're eating the earth."

"What are they digging for?" he asked.

"*Des diamants,*" Zuzu replied under her breath.

Amber sighed in dismay. "All that destruction for a diamond ring!"

"*C'est le Black Mamba!*" hissed Zuzu, ducking down.

Connor followed her line of sight and spotted a large man in army fatigues. Even from a distance, the infamous warlord struck an imposing figure. Barrel-chested and with bulging muscles, General Pascal towered over his fellow rebel soldiers, even Blaze, whom Connor easily recognized from the flash of his mirrored sunglasses. So his hunch had been right: the Armée Nationale de la Liberté had ambushed the president and his entourage.

By the look of deep-set fear on Zuzu's face, Connor's suspicions about her trustworthiness were allayed. She seemed only too aware of the rebel leader's reputation as a cold-blooded murderer of women and children.

"*C'est trop dangereux ici!*" she was saying, pulling at Amber's arm to leave.

Amber shook her head. "*Non! D'abord nous devons trouver Henri.*"

Scanning the rebel camp, Connor began to search for her brother among the groups of bone-tired, mud-smeared workers. If Blaze was here, there was a strong chance Henri would be too.

"There he is!" he gasped, pointing past a sad collection

of canvas shelters to a waiflike boy staggering across the rocky riverbed. Henri's red hair and pale skin made him easily identifiable among the other enslaved workers as he struggled to carry a heavy bucket of soil. After stumbling a few more feet, he dropped the bucket, hunching over, clearly fighting for breath.

"He needs his inhaler," cried Amber, her fingers clutching at the medicine in her pocket.

Then they watched in horror as the boy soldier with the red beret—No Mercy, as Blaze had called him—strode over and raised a bamboo cane high above Henri's head. Henri cowered at the threat, picked up the bucket and tottered a few more paces before collapsing again.

"He could *die* if they force him to go on," said Amber, her face paling in shock at the state of her brother.

As No Mercy began to beat Henri with the cane, she let out a stifled cry and rose from behind their hiding place.

"No!" hissed Connor, grabbing her arm and pulling her back down. He pointed to a rebel soldier standing guard on an outcrop of rock farther down the slope. "We wait until dark."

35

Connor peered through the undergrowth at the rebels' camp. In the pale light of a waning moon, he spotted several guards patrolling the perimeter, their weapons slung lazily over their shoulders. The rest of General Pascal's soldiers were gathered around glaringly bright kerosene lamps, playing cards, joking and laughing. A row of canvas tents formed the center of the camp from which hip-hop music blared out of a portable speaker, the heavy beat pulsating through the valley. Farther downstream, fires dotted the ravaged banks of the river where clusters of enslaved workers lay exhausted beneath ragged canvas shelters.

That was where Henri would most likely be. If he was still alive.

The hours to dusk had been the longest Connor had ever experienced in his lifetime. The image of Henri being beaten and forced to work while fighting for breath had played over and over in his mind. But he knew that striding into the rebels' camp in broad daylight would have been tantamount to signing their own death warrants. So they'd descended partway back down the hillside to bide their time, Zuzu cooking the dik-dik straight on the embers of an open fire for an early dinner while Amber sat silent, her knees clasped to her chest.

As soon as the sun had dropped below the horizon, the three of them returned to the hilltop, then worked their way down into the hidden valley. Zuzu had been careful to avoid any rebel lookouts, a task made easier as the light rapidly faded. But this also meant the jungle trails were now pitch-black, making the route treacherous underfoot, and Connor doubted they'd have reached the bottom of the valley without Zuzu to guide them.

"Can you see Henri?" whispered Amber, who crouched next to Connor in the darkness, Zuzu on his other side.

Connor shook his head. "Stay here. I'll find him."

"Don't forget this," said Amber, passing him the inhaler. As he took it from her, she gave his hand an anxious squeeze.

"Don't worry," he assured her. "I'll get him back, I promise."

As he was rising, Zuzu tapped him on the shoulder and signed for him to wait. Scooping up some mud, she smeared his face and arms until his skin was all but blackened. *"Camouflage,"* she whispered.

"Good thinking," he replied.

Connor waited for a guard to go by, then crept from the

cover of the bushes and into the rebels' camp. His heart raced as he clambered down the riverbank. With nothing to hide him but the moonlit darkness and his improvised camouflage, Connor felt very exposed and prayed he wouldn't be spotted. The riverbed was a patchwork of puddles and pits, loose gravel and thick mud. His boots sank into the soft ground, slowing his progress, and he was still making his way across when a boy soldier suddenly appeared on the opposite bank. Connor dropped into a shallow pit, flattening himself in the dirt as the boy approached. The rebel stopped only a few feet away from where Connor was hiding.

Had the boy seen him?

Connor pressed himself farther into the earth, his heart in his mouth as he waited for the alarm to be raised or a gun to be put to his head. A still-glowing cigarette butt landed by his face, ashes spurting into his eyes. Connor tried not to cough as acrid smoke wafted up his nostrils. Blinking away the ash, he glanced up, half expecting to see the boy's face leering down at him, but all he could hear was the splash of water as the soldier relieved himself before heading back along the bank to rejoin his companions.

Breathing a sigh of relief, Connor crawled out of the pit. Crouching low, he darted up the bank and over to a pile of earth near the workers' encampment. It was truly hell on earth. The flickering fires illuminated the haggard faces of men and children, half dead from exhaustion and hunger, their eyes sunken and their cheeks hollow. The smell of stale sweat from days of hard labor was thick in the air, along with the stench of human waste from the nearby bushes.

Connor ducked down as another guard strolled past. For no apparent reason, the soldier kicked one of the sleeping workers in the gut. As his victim groaned in shock and pain, the soldier walked off, chuckling to himself. Connor realized more than ever that he had to get Henri out. The boy wouldn't last another day under such treatment.

He finally spotted Henri, slightly apart from the other men at the back of one of the shelters. He was curled up in the fetal position, his body trembling like a leaf, his strained wheezing for breath cutting through the ragged snores of the other workers.

Silently Connor crept around, keeping to the shadows and away from the light of the fires. Kneeling beside Henri, he placed a gentle hand on the boy's shoulder and a finger to his lips. Henri flinched and his eyes widened in horror.

"It's me, Connor," he whispered, realizing his camouflaged face must look nightmarish to the poor traumatized boy.

"They said . . . you were dead," he rasped.

"Well, I'm not. And neither is your sister."

It took a moment for this to sink in, and then Henri managed a weak smile. Connor produced the inhaler and helped Henri with it. After a minute or so, his breathing hadn't eased, so he administered two more doses until gradually the wheezing subsided. Although Henri needed more time to recover, Connor couldn't risk delaying much longer. A guard could pass by at any second.

"Can you walk?" he whispered.

Henri nodded. As Connor pulled him into a sitting position, one of the workers opened his eyes and looked directly at them. Connor froze, waiting to see what the man's reaction would be.

"*C'est mon ami,*" Henri explained.

The man winked, as if to say their secret was safe with him, and closed his eyes again.

Henri winced as Connor dragged him to his feet.

"I'm okay," he whispered, putting on a brave face.

Connor could feel the crisscross of raised welts that the bamboo cane had inflicted upon his body and realized that Henri must be in excruciating pain. Admiring the boy's courage, he gently placed Henri's arm over his shoulder and helped him toward the river. As they stumbled through the dug-out pits and waterlogged ditches, Connor glanced back to make sure there were no guards in sight. Thankfully the rebels still appeared to be absorbed in their card games. Helping Henri up the opposite bank, Connor knew they were going to make it.

They were almost within reach of the cover of the bushes when there was a shout. All of a sudden flashlight beams cut through the darkness like swords. More shouts broke out, and for a moment Connor believed they'd been spotted.

But the alarm hadn't been raised for them.

Farther upstream Amber was being frog-marched into the rebel camp at gunpoint.

36

Connor bundled Henri into the bushes. They charged along a trail, foliage slapping at their faces in the pitch-darkness. Gunfire roared and the jungle erupted around them, tracer bullets shredding leaves and pulverizing tree trunks. As they ducked the gunfire, Henri's foot snagged on a root and they both tumbled to the ground. The shouts of the rebels closed in on them. Winded, Connor hauled Henri back to his feet and they stumbled on blindly.

Connor cursed his luck. He was back to square one, having swapped one Principal for the other. *But how was Amber caught?*

Zuzu must have betrayed them. He realized her superstition about the hill and her fearful reaction to the Black Mamba had merely been an act. He *should* have trusted his gut instinct and overruled Amber, making sure they returned to the lodge.

But it was too late for hindsight and regret. The jungle

was swarming with rebels, and survival was all that counted.

Soldiers crashed through the bushes to the right and left of them, bursts of gunfire lighting up the darkness like fire-crackers. Connor, however, sensed some chaos in the rebels' movements. Their search seemed too widespread and too random for them to be hunting him and Henri specifically. Connor guessed that they didn't yet know Henri was miss-ing and so the mobilization of soldiers was just a knee-jerk reaction to an unexpected intruder. This might play to their advantage if they could find a place to hide and wait out the haphazard search.

As they scrambled up a slope, they passed an old tree with a hollowed-out trunk.

"In there," Connor instructed, hoping no poisonous in-sects or snakes had made it their home.

Henri knelt down and looked inside. "But it's not big enough for us both."

"It doesn't need to be. I'm going to rescue your sister."

Henri's eyes widened. "How?"

"I haven't figured that out yet. But I need you hidden from the rebels to do so."

Henri reluctantly crawled inside the hollow. Connor covered the entrance with fallen branches and leaves. It wouldn't fool a tracker, but at night it disguised the hole well enough to pass a cursory inspection.

Henri peered out. "You won't leave me here, will you?"

Connor shook his head. "No—but if for any reason I'm not back by dawn, head south to the lodge."

Connor could see this prospect terrified the boy. Removing his Rangeman watch, Connor reached in and attached it to Henri's wrist. "Press here for the compass," he explained. "It was a special birthday present, so take good care of it until I return."

Henri nodded, the responsibility of the watch appearing to give him some comfort, or at least a sense of purpose.

With a final check that the hole was completely hidden, Connor doubled back down the trail, being careful to avoid detection by the soldiers still scouring the jungle around him. His aim was to infiltrate their line and find a concealed spot on the riverbank from which to locate Amber. After that—

The barrel of an AK-47 materialized from the darkness and was thrust into Connor's face.

"Don't shoot!" he cried, holding up his hands as the boy in the red beret began to squeeze the trigger.

37

His eyes flickering open, Connor found himself staring into the face of death for a second time that night. He'd seen it first when the boy soldier had pressed the cold steel barrel of the AK-47 against his forehead. Believing his life to be over, a nightmarish vision had flashed before him until, at the very last second, No Mercy had released the pressure on the rifle's trigger. Instead Connor had received a brutal blow to the jaw with the gun's stock. When he came to, Connor was confronted by death again. But this time the face was real. Black as coal, with pockmarked skin and fathomless eyes as inhuman as a snake's, it glared at him with cruel, hard intent.

"Où est le garçon?" it asked him.

In his dazed state, Connor didn't answer. His lack of response resulted in a savage slap across his cheek, the blow so hard, his head rang like a bell. Blinking back tears of pain, he tried to focus on his tormentor's face. He was almost blinded by the harsh light from a kerosene lamp, and then the Black Mamba himself swam into his vision.

"*Où est le garçon?*" General Pascal repeated.

"I . . . don't understand," Connor murmured.

"*Anglais!*" he remarked, raising an eyebrow in surprise. He switched to a heavily accented English. "Where's the boy?"

"What boy?" Connor replied.

The general struck him again. Stars flared before his eyes and Connor tasted blood as his lip split. But he'd been knocked around enough in kickboxing class to be able to take a few blows.

"The diplomat's son. Or do you need another reminder?" The general raised his hand again to strike.

Bracing himself for the inevitable pain, Connor didn't even flinch at the threat. But rather than hit him, General Pascal broke into a broad grin. "I like this one. He's got spirit," he announced to the soldiers encircling them. The general turned back to Connor, propped up against a rock in the heart of the rebel camp. "It's no matter. We'll find the boy in the morning. I hear from Blaze you're quite a fighter. Defeating *two* of my soldiers."

Connor glanced over and spotted the rebel he'd kicked into the wait-a-while bush. The man's face, arms and legs were lacerated with small weeping cuts. Beside him stood Dredd, his mauled arm hanging useless in a bloody bandage at his side, but at least he was alive.

"Let's have some sport, boys," declared General Pascal. "I want to see this White Warrior in action for myself. Hornet!"

He beckoned over a boy soldier wearing a blue New Orleans Hornets T-shirt. Thickset with a heavy brow and a permanent scowl, the boy matched Connor for height but easily outgunned him in the muscle department. He looked like he'd been raised on a diet of buffalo and pure brutality.

"Let's see how you fare against my champion."

"I don't want to fight him," said Connor tiredly, aware he probably didn't have much choice in the matter.

The general jutted his chin in the direction of Blaze, who stepped into the circle of light, dragging Amber with him. She appeared shaken but unhurt.

"Connor!" she gasped, rushing forward.

But Blaze yanked her back, unsheathed his machete and held the blade to her throat.

General Pascal grinned at Connor. "Is that enough incentive for you?"

38

A ring of kerosene lamps marked the boundary of the dug-out pit, casting a bright stadium-like glow over the water-logged ground. Rebel soldiers jostled for position on the edge, eager for a good view of the impending death match between Hornet and the White Warrior.

Connor glanced up at the hostile crowd. He'd experienced some tough bouts in his rise to becoming UK Junior Kickboxing Champion, but this made each and every one of them seem like a playground fight by comparison.

On the opposite side of the pit, Hornet pulled off his T-shirt to reveal a rippling six-pack and a multitude of scars, clear evidence that he was a hardened fighter. In his injured and exhausted state, Connor realized his chances of defeating the boy were close to zero. But he refused to let himself think like that. His kickboxing trainer, Dan, had instilled in him an indomitable fighting spirit: *The will to win is the way to win.*

Connor went through his pre-match rituals, shaking his limbs loose, stretching and bringing his mind into sharp focus. He knew he couldn't conquer his opponent through strength, so he'd have to be quicker, more agile and more cunning in his fight strategy. He needed to end it fast and hard.

"This isn't a dance!" shouted one of the boy soldiers as Connor limbered up his legs. The crowd burst into mocking laughter.

Connor ignored the heckle and called up to General Pascal, reclined in a deck chair at the edge of the ring as if he were some Roman emperor. "What if I beat your champion?"

Glugging from a bottle, General Pascal snorted in amusement. "*If* you win, I'll let the girl go. If you don't, then"—the general shrugged—"you won't be in any state to care what happens to her."

Amber stared down at Connor in mute terror as Blaze ran the back edge of his machete across her cheek, goading Connor to react. But this threat to Amber's life only strengthened Connor's resolve to fight to his dying breath to save her.

"Let the battle begin!" General Pascal announced, raising his bottle in a salute.

Like a pack of ravenous hyenas, the crowd whooped and whistled their approval.

Hornet roared straight in, charging across the pit like a bull elephant. Connor stood his ground, poised on the balls of his feet, waiting for the exact moment to make his move. Hornet lowered his head, turning it into a battering ram that would flatten a tank. At the last second Connor sidestepped the boy and simultaneously directed a hammer-fist strike to the base of his skull, targeting a knockout pressure point just below the right ear.

Hornet went down as hard and heavy as the buffalo that the Wolf had shot. He slumped face-first in the mud. The whooping crowd fell silent, shocked at the impossibly swift defeat of their champion. Then they began to jeer.

"I win," declared Connor.

General Pascal smiled knowingly. "I don't think so," he replied, pointing in the direction of his fallen soldier. "All you've done is make him angry."

Connor turned to see Hornet up on his feet, shaking his head clear and back on the attack. Yelling a battle cry, he swung a sledgehammer of a fist at Connor's head. With barely time to duck, Connor stepped forward and drove a vertical punch into the boy's solar plexus. Grunting from the force of the blow, Hornet grew more furious and elbowed Connor in the jaw. Already weakened from No Mercy's assault with his AK-47, Connor was momentarily stunned and reeled away as Hornet pressed his advantage and launched a blistering attack. He hook-punched Connor in the gut, then pummeled him in the lower ribs. Connor gasped as a fist struck home and opened up his stitched wound. Hornet saw the increased flare of pain in Connor's eyes and struck again.

As the boy pounded him with relentless fury, the soldiers surrounding the pit began to chant, *"Hornet! Hornet! Hornet!"*

Forced to retreat from the onslaught, Connor soon found himself up against the wall of rebels. They pushed him back into the pit. Hornet was waiting for him. He grabbed Connor, lifted him high in the air, then brought him crashing down into a large pool of muddy water. Connor crumpled like a rag doll. Hornet dropped on top of him and shoved his head beneath the surface.

Cut off from air, Connor struggled in the boy's merciless grip. The shouts of the crowd became distorted and his mouth flooded with marshy water. Briefly his head came up, and as he snatched a desperate breath, he heard Amber screaming his name above the baying of the crowd. Then Hornet forced him back under.

Spluttering and blinded, Connor tried to buck his attacker off. But Hornet was simply too heavy and too strong. Feeling his own strength fading fast, Connor knew he was in a fight to the death. In a last-ditch attempt to free himself, he reached behind for Hornet's inner thigh and pinched the *yako* nerve point.

Nothing happened.

Connor squeezed harder. But Hornet kept him pinned under the water. Perhaps the boy was tougher than Dredd, but Connor had seen Ling use the exact same nerve point on a two-hundred-pound hit man, and that guy had leaped away as if electrocuted. For some unexplained reason, Hornet was immune to the technique.

Connor clawed at the mud around him, trying to pull himself free. His hand came across a stone. He grabbed it and, in a final act of survival, smashed the rock down on his attacker's bare foot. Hornet let out a grunt of pain. Connor struck again. This time he heard a sickening crack of bones and Hornet released his grip, rolling away in agony.

The crowd booed as Connor clambered back to his feet. However, by the time he turned around to confront his opponent, Hornet had limped over to the edge of the pit and picked up a shovel.

Wielding the shovel like a weapon, he snarled, "Time to dig your grave!"

Connor instinctively reached for his father's knife on his hip, but discovered it was missing. From the sidelines, No Mercy waved the knife teasingly at him.

Hornet swung the shovel. Connor leaped back as the metal edge almost sliced him in half, then ducked as the shovel came back at him. Hornet roared in frustrated anger and brought the shovel arcing down toward Connor's head. With nowhere left to retreat, Connor had to dive to one side. As he rolled back to his feet, Hornet took another swing and the shovel hit him square in the back. Connor went down as if he'd been hit by a bus.

Winded and in pain, he crawled away through the mud. Hornet bore down on him, raising the shovel to land the killing blow. In that moment, Connor realized it was all over.

Then he heard Amber scream, *"Behind you!"*

Connor glanced over his shoulder. A metal panning sieve lay discarded at the edge of the pit. It would have been out of his reach, except that the boy soldier Dredd had casually kicked it down the slope to him. A small gesture for the life debt he owed Connor.

Connor seized it and held it over himself as a shield. Hornet's shovel clashed loudly against the metal pan. Infuriated, he struck again. Connor deflected the blow, then kicked out with all his might at Hornet's knee. There was an excruciating crunch and the boy staggered backward, screaming in pain.

Leaping up, Connor smashed the shovel from Hornet's grip with the pan, then caught him across the jaw with it. Discarding the pan, he locked his hands around the dazed boy's neck and yanked him down hard onto his driving knee. Blood spurted from Hornet's flattened nose. Connor repeated the knee strike over and over, knocking the boy senseless. When his opponent's legs went from under him, he released his grip and let Hornet collapse in the mud. Fueled by rage and the instinct to survive at all costs, Connor now picked up the shovel and lifted it high above his head to strike a final blow. Crippled and half unconscious, Hornet held up a hand in a pitiful attempt to defend himself.

"Kill! Kill! Kill!" chanted the soldiers, caught up in the bloodlust.

Connor hesitated only briefly, then brought the shovel down with all his strength, striking a rock beside Hornet's head.

There was a groan of disappointment from the crowd.

"How could he miss?" cried one of the soldiers.

Weary and battle worn, Connor tossed the shovel aside. "I don't kill," he said, more to himself than the rebel crowd. "I protect."

39

Connor stood defiant before General Pascal. "You promised to let Amber go."

The general tossed his empty bottle into the pit and smirked at him. "Only if you won."

Gloating at Connor's indignant and crestfallen expression, Blaze kept holding the machete to Amber's throat.

"But I defeated your champion!" Connor protested, pointing to the groaning Hornet being borne away by his fellow soldiers.

"No, you lost," declared the general. He stabbed a finger in Connor's chest. "Showing mercy makes you weak. Only the death of your enemy makes you a true victor. But you will learn that—in time."

"What do you mean?"

General Pascal's eyes twinkled. "You're *my* White Warrior now."

Connor stared at him in disbelief. "I'll never fight for you."

The general laughed. "But you just did!"

"No, I fought for Amber's freedom."

General Pascal laughed. "How romantic. For that gesture, I'll let her live. But only for as long as you remain my champion."

He turned his attention to Amber. Stroking a lock of her fine hair between his fingers, he mused, "Maybe I could take this flame-haired beauty for my wife?"

Connor felt his blood start to boil.

"Oh, don't worry, my White Warrior. I'll take *good* care of her."

The general looked to Blaze. "Tie them both up. We don't want them running away. And in the morning hunt down her baby brother. I want that little rat back in its trap."

Blaze sheathed his machete with a growl of disappointment and ordered No Mercy over. "Help me secure these two," he muttered.

With a gun to his back, Connor realized that any further resistance was futile. As the two of them were roughly manhandled over to a stand of trees, Connor caught a faint whiff of expensive aftershave. The scent was out of place among these unwashed rebels, and he looked sharply around. Just beyond the light of the kerosene lamps, a man stood in the shadows. It was too dark to make him out, but General Pascal had walked over to talk with the mysterious stranger.

As Blaze and No Mercy bound them, Connor strained to hear their conversation.

"... keeping these children captive could draw unwanted international attention," the man was saying.

"Why? They'll be presumed dead in the ambush," replied the general. "Besides, the boy has great potential."

"I don't care what you do with them," said the man. "Just make sure they never leave this valley alive."

40

Broken, beaten and bleeding, Connor bowed his head in defeat. Bound to the trunk of a tree, the prisoner of a crazed rebel tyrant and lost to the outside world, he knew their fate was all but sealed. By now Guardian would be going into overdrive to locate him and his Principals. But what hope did they have of finding them in a hidden valley in a country soon to be torn apart by civil war? General Pascal could spirit them away into the jungle at a moment's notice. Or kill and bury them at the first sign of a rescue attempt.

No Mercy stood guard a short distance away, playfully flipping Connor's knife in his hand. Connor watched bitterly as the blade twirled and glinted in the light of a kerosene lamp. He could hear his father's voice ordering him to *never give in, never give up.* However, confronted with the harsh reality of their situation, he couldn't even hold on to the slightest shred of hope. His spirits were at their lowest ebb, lost in a pit of despair. He'd given his all to protect Amber and Henri, but in the end it hadn't been enough.

"Are you okay?" whispered Amber. She was slumped in the dirt beside him, her arms lashed behind her back to the opposite tree.

Connor raised his lolling head. "I've been better," he replied, attempting a smile, but even that hurt.

Amber looked his battered body over with sad, guilt-ridden eyes. "I'm . . . so sorry," she said, weeping.

"For what?" he murmured.

"For getting us into this mess. For the pain you've gone through trying to protect me." The tears now flowed freely down her dirt-stained cheeks. "You were right. We should have gone back to the lodge. Contacted help. I don't know what I was thinking. I was just so desperate to get Henri back. This is all my fault—"

"No, it's not," Connor cut in. "I made the decision to come here. It was my duty to protect *both* of you."

Amber gazed at him with deep affection. "And you did rescue my brother. For that, I'll be grateful for the rest of my life . . . however long that might be," she added with a weak smile.

Connor's thoughts went to Henri hiding alone in the dark hollow of the tree, waiting for their return. A return that would never happen. He prayed the boy would leave at first light, before the rebels began their search. Otherwise their sacrifice would have been for nothing.

"How did you get caught, by the way?" Connor asked Amber.

"A guard sneaked up on me from behind."

"What happened to Zuzu?"

Amber shrugged. "When the soldier grabbed me, I looked around, but she was gone."

"So, do you think she betrayed us?" said Connor, the girl's deception leaving a sour taste in his mouth.

"I guess she must have," Amber said, sighing. "How else would the guard have known where I was?"

In the distance, a flash of forked lightning lit up the pitch-black sky. The lone acacia tree atop the peak was starkly visible for a brief second, appearing like a warped gallows before plunging back into darkness. As the bleak image faded, and Connor and Amber resigned themselves to their inevitable fate, a long, low ominous rumble thundered overhead.

41

Alpha team fell silent as Colonel Black marched into the operations room. The stiff measured stride and grim expression on his face told them he wasn't delivering good news.

"Take a seat, everyone," he instructed, his voice rough from a night of no sleep.

Exchanging anxious looks, they hurried to their places. Charley rolled to the front, braced for the worst.

"This is the situation," said the colonel. "The Burundian president has been assassinated in an ambush. The army found the remnants of his safari convoy in sector four of the park, some twenty miles from the lodge."

Colonel Black tapped a command on his tablet computer. Wirelessly linked to the wide-screen wall monitors, a satellite image of a dried-out riverbed appeared on the display. The resolution was low, but the scene was clear enough. Four immobilized vehicles, one of which was overturned and burned out, another no more than a smoking charred shell. A bomb crater from a rocket-propelled grenade was also visible.

"What are the dark blobs?" asked Jason, squinting at the screen.

"Bodies," replied the colonel.

The mood of the room dropped another notch.

"Are there . . . *any* survivors?" asked Charley.

The colonel nodded. "The major general reports that two ministers and their wives were rescued from the lodge, where they were being held prisoner by members of the Armée Nationale de la Liberté led by General Pascal, aka the Black Mamba."

"But what about Connor and the Barbier family?" pressed Ling.

"That we don't know," the colonel admitted with a heavy sigh. "The ambush site is still being investigated by the army. If they were in one of the burned-out vehicles, it'll take some time to identify the bodies."

Choking back her rising emotion, Charley asked, "Don't the survivors know what happened to them?"

"Not according to the major general. The ministers fled during the initial phase of the ambush only to be caught later. There is some hope, though. One of the Land Rovers from the safari convoy is missing."

"So you think Connor may have gotten away?" questioned Richie.

"That's the scenario I'd like to believe. And the one we're going to work to. However, forty-eight hours have passed since the ambush with no communication from Connor. From that, we can presume four possibilities: one, he's in hiding; two, he has since been captured; three, he is lying injured somewhere; or, worst-case scenario, he's . . ." The colonel didn't need to finish the sentence for Alpha team to guess the fourth and final possibility.

"So what's the plan?" asked Ling.

"The Burundian army has taken back the lodge from the rebels," Colonel Black explained. "The major general is sending in reinforcements, and his army has begun a sector-by-sector search of the park. If Connor or any of the Barbiers are still alive, they'll find them."

Charley raised her hand. "I think one of the team needs to fly out there and help with the search."

"I agree," said the colonel.

"Then I volunteer."

Colonel Black emphatically shook his head.

Charley frowned at him. "Is it because I'm in a wheelchair you won't send me?"

The colonel shot her an affronted look. "I appreciate you're upset, Charley, but you know me better than that. The fact is I wouldn't send *any* of you to a country that's on the verge of a civil war."

"But we *need* somebody on the ground," Charley insisted.

"You're not going and that's an order."

"So who is going?" asked Jason.

"I am."

The colonel handed out folders as he headed for the door. "Here are your individual tasks. I depart in one hour for Burundi and want updates from all of you by the time I leave."

As Alpha team digested their assignments, Charley stared at the satellite image of the burned-out vehicles surrounded by countless dark blobs. She wiped away a tear with the back of her hand.

"Don't worry," said Ling, putting an arm around her. "Connor's a survivor."

42

Sometime during the night, the first drops of rain fell on Connor's face. It was cool and refreshing, and he let the drops roll down his cheeks. As the rain intensified, he opened his mouth, relishing the life-giving water. Then the shower became a torrential downpour, drumming on the tree canopy overhead and drowning out all other noise. The layers of dirt and blood were washed from his skin and clothes, his wounds cleansed and his body partly revived.

The rebels hurried to the shelter of their tents while the enslaved workers shivered and shook out in the open, their canvas roofs having collapsed under the sheer weight of the water. The stand of trees Connor and Amber were tied under offered scant protection from the storm, and exposed to its full might, they too began shuddering from the rain-drenched cold.

With the guards huddling in their tents and the kerosene lamps guttering in the deluge, Connor realized that this was their best, and possibly only, opportunity to escape. But try as he might, he couldn't free his hands. He thought the rain might help him slip out of his bindings, but the wet rope had swelled up and was now even tighter around his wrists. Connor struggled until exhaustion overwhelmed him.

He must have drifted off, because the next thing he heard was a massive explosion and the distinctive *crack* of gunfire. The rain still fell in sheets, but a pale pre-dawn light was now battling to push through the tail end of the storm. Throughout the camp, rebels were snatching up weapons and firing indiscriminately into the surrounding jungle. Another explosion ripped through the valley as a mortar detonated in the riverbed, sending up a shower of dirt and debris. The enslaved workers ran for cover, but many were cut down by gunfire from the bushes.

"What's happening?" cried Amber, her wet hair matted to her face.

"It must be the army," Connor replied. "Somehow they've found us!"

"Then we're saved?" She seemed not to know whether to laugh or cry with joy at the news.

But Connor realized this was no time to rejoice. They were stuck in the heart of the kill zone, at risk from both rebel *and* friendly fire. Whether rescue was coming or not, Connor knew they had to A-C-E it out of the camp as fast as possible. *Assess the threat. Counter the danger. Escape the kill zone.* Otherwise they'd be slaughtered like the rest of the workers.

He renewed his effort to free his hands, the skin around his wrists scraped raw as he twisted and pulled. Amid the chaos of the surprise attack, General Pascal barked orders to his rebel army of men and boy soldiers. Despite despising the rebel leader to his very core, Connor couldn't deny the man's military expertise. Honed through years of guerrilla warfare in the jungle, the general quickly rallied his troops into several cohesive fighting units, then launched a counteroffensive against the enemy hidden in the forested slopes of the valley.

As he commanded his forces, the general shouted at No Mercy to keep guard over Connor and Amber, giving the boy soldier express orders to kill them if any government soldiers entered the rebel camp.

Connor yanked harder on his bindings, but still they wouldn't give. Amber was struggling too.

No Mercy sneered at their pathetic attempts and, after making sure the knots were still secure, turned his attention to the firefight raging all around them. Tracer bullets zipped overhead, and another mortar exploded nearby, destroying a rebel tent. Screams of wounded men filled the air. As debris and shrapnel rained down on them, No Mercy unleashed the full force of his AK-47 at the first of the government troops advancing from the bushes.

With the boy distracted, Connor drew on all his strength and tugged at his bindings with every fiber of his body. The rope didn't give an inch. Infuriated, he yanked again and again.

Then, when he'd given up all hope, the rope unexpectedly snapped.

Connor jumped up and seized No Mercy in a rear chokehold, a classic jujitsu technique used to subdue an opponent. Unable to breathe and with the blood flow to his brain cut off, No Mercy struggled violently to free himself. But in less than ten seconds he fell limp in Connor's grip. Despite the boy's merciless nature, Connor had no desire to kill him or leave him brain damaged. So he immediately released the choke and let the boy collapse, unconscious, to the muddy ground.

Recovering his father's knife, Connor raced over to Amber and cut her bonds. It took several slices, and Connor was amazed that he'd managed to snap his own bindings. As soon as she was free, Amber grabbed hold of him in relief, her body trembling like a sparrow's. Then she suddenly stiffened and Connor turned his head to see General Pascal standing over them, his Glock 17 handgun aimed squarely at his back.

"You certainly live up to your name, White Warrior," declared the general, glancing down at the inert body of the boy soldier. "And you will die by it too."

43

An arrow flew out of nowhere, piercing General Pascal's fore-arm and throwing off his aim. He screamed in agony and fury as the round he'd shot missed its target and obliterated the bark beside Connor's head. His gun slipping from his grip, the general clasped his injured arm, blood spurting from the wound as he yelled to his soldiers for assistance.

Before reinforcements could come to the general's aid, Connor pulled Amber to her feet and they both fled. Only now did Connor catch a glimpse of what had actually bro-ken his own bindings. A second arrow was embedded in the trunk of his tree, the sharpened tip having severed the rope in two.

On the other side of the riverbed, concealed among the bushes, Zuzu urgently beckoned Connor and Amber across. As she loosed another arrow at a rebel trying to stop them, Connor rebuked himself for having thought the girl had betrayed them. He vowed to buy her a whole wardrobe of clothes if they ever got out of this valley alive!

Behind them, the Black Mamba was bellowing his rage above the noise of the firefight and relentless rain. *"Stop them!"*

Glancing back over his shoulder, Connor spotted several soldiers sprinting after them with the machete-wielding Blaze, his murderous intent clear in the bloodlust set of his eyes. Pushing Amber ahead, Connor followed her down the slippery bank. The storm had turned the riverbed into a quagmire, and they found themselves knee-deep in mud and water. As they waded across the boggy terrain, the rebels rapidly closed in.

After taking two more of the soldiers down, Zuzu had run out of arrows and could only urge them on from the bushes. Then she started to shout and point manically upstream. Hearing an ominous rumble, Connor turned to see a wall of brown foaming water thundering down the riverbed. The makeshift dam had burst, and a flash flood was sweeping through the valley.

"Go! Go!" Connor screamed at Amber.

They tried to increase their pace, but the ground sucked at their feet, seemingly intent on holding them in the path of the oncoming flood. Confronted by such a terrifying force of nature, their pursuers gave up the chase and turned back.

Flinging themselves forward, Connor and Amber reached the opposite bank and desperately clawed their way up. But the slick mud made the slope treacherous, and they slipped back down. The flood was almost on top of them when Zuzu raced over and pulled Amber to safety. Connor felt the ground washed from under his feet. Then his legs were whipped away. Zuzu and Amber grabbed for his outstretched arms. The bushgirl missed, but Amber managed to clasp his trailing hand. She dug her heels into the mud as the current threatened to drag Connor away and her back in.

"Stay with me!" Amber cried as she felt his fingers slipping from her grasp.

Connor strained with all his might to hold on, but the flood seemed determined to claim him. Zuzu now wrapped her arms around Amber's waist in a frantic tug-of-war for Connor's life. With a final desperate pull, they hauled him clear from the torrent of debris, water and rocks hurtling past.

"Thanks," Connor gasped as the two girls helped him to his feet. "That was a *close* call!"

On the other side of the churning river, Blaze was also dragging himself out, plunging his machete deep into the mud as an anchor. But the other soldiers weren't so fortunate and were borne away, screaming, on the tide of foaming water.

Zuzu tugged on Connor's elbow, urging him and Amber to leave, but Connor was rooted to the spot.

"Let's go!" implored Amber, but then she saw the pale, wide-eyed expression on his face. "What's the matter? You look like you've seen a ghost."

"*I have*," he said, his reply barely more than a whisper.

Through the haze of falling rain, Connor saw an ashen-faced man with eyes of death and a stillness that was disturbing amid the chaos and destruction of the battle and the flood. A deep shudder ran through Connor at the ghostly vision. He'd met this man once before—upon a burning tanker off the coast of Somalia. He'd been presumed dead, no trace of him having ever been found. Now that very same man stood on the opposite bank, staring directly at Connor.

The man raised his semi-automatic pistol and took careful aim. Connor instinctively ducked. A bullet shot past his ear. There was a scream of pain. Connor spun, expecting to see Amber or Zuzu lying dead in the mud. But it was a rebel soldier who'd been killed.

Not waiting for the ghost from his past to take another shot, Connor fled with the two girls into the jungle.

44

Connor ripped aside the clump of foliage but found nothing. It was the wrong tree. He went from one trunk to the other, searching for the hollow where he'd hidden Henri. But the jungle had looked completely different during the night, and he was now totally disoriented. "I know it's around here somewhere," he assured Amber.

The sound of gunfire was drawing ever closer. Zuzu pleaded with them to keep moving.

Torn between locating her brother and taking Zuzu's advice, Amber questioned, "Will he still even be there? You told him to leave at first light."

"I know," Connor replied, their search becoming more and more desperate. "But we *have* to check in case he stayed behind."

"Maybe the army has found him," said Amber hopefully.

A hand grenade detonated close by and they all dropped

to the ground, burning leaves and scorched earth raining down on them.

"You go with Zuzu," Connor ordered Amber, their ears ringing from the blast. "I'll find your brother."

Amber shook her head. "No, we stick together."

"You don't have a choice," said Connor, dragging her to her feet. "I'm not risking you getting caught again. Now go with Zu—"

"*Connor! Amber!*" a voice hissed.

They both spun around. Farther up the slope, a pair of scared eyes peeked out from behind a thick layer of leaves and branches. Connor had concealed the hollow's entrance far better than he'd ever imagined.

"Henri!" Amber cried, scrambling up the slope and pulling away the branches. Henri crawled out and Amber embraced him so hard, Connor thought she'd never let go.

"Sorry, Connor," Henri mumbled, his face pressed against his sister's chest. "I was too scared to leave with all the fighting."

Connor smiled kindly. "It's a good thing you didn't; otherwise—"

"*Allons-y!*" called Zuzu, frantically beckoning them to follow her.

"But the lodge is that way," Connor argued, pointing upslope.

Zuzu vehemently shook her head and rattled off some French at him.

"When two elephants fight, it's the grass that gets trampled," Amber interpreted, finally relinquishing her grip on her brother. "She says it's safer to go the long way around. Avoid the fighting."

As another grenade exploded off to their left, Connor didn't need any further convincing. They dashed along an animal trail, following the course of the river. With every step they took farther down the valley, the sounds of battle gradually receded and the rain began to ease. Zuzu slowed their pace a little, allowing Henri to grab a couple of puffs from his inhaler. By the time they reached the drop-off at the end of the valley, the storm had passed and dawn's light had broken through the clouds in golden rays.

They stopped at the edge of the waterfall, its glistening curtain cascading down one hundred and fifty feet to a large natural pool below. From their viewpoint looking out across the park, Connor was once again astounded at the majestic beauty of Africa. The rolling savannah, fresh with rain, appeared to have reawakened. The trees and bushland had taken on a lusher shade of green and seemingly blossomed overnight. Birds sang a mellifluous chorus as they fluttered and swooped in the crystal-clear air. On the plain, herds of zebra, antelope and wildebeest grazed in countless numbers, braying and snorting, while a parade of mighty elephants strode toward the Ruvubu River, grown pregnant with floodwaters and now sparkling like a jeweled ribbon in the early morning light.

The storm had brought more than rain—it had brought life.

Amber peered over the lip of the waterfall, then glanced at Connor. "No jumping this time," she said, the corner of her lips turning up into a teasing smile. "We climb down."

"Fine by me," he replied.

Moving carefully along the slippery rock, Amber picked the easiest route down the face, following a natural fault line. It was slow going, but the handholds were positive and plentiful, and they all reached the bottom safely. From the pool, Zuzu guided them along the line of the tributary river through the trees toward the plain. Connor took up the rear, ensuring they weren't being followed. No one talked, all of them shattered and shell-shocked from their harrowing night and fraught escape.

Up ahead, Zuzu came to a sudden halt. Amber asked in a whisper what was wrong. Zuzu put a finger to her lips and unsheathed her knife.

The birds had stopped singing in their part of the jungle.

45

Connor sensed the danger too. He felt eyes upon them. Watchful and waiting. Drawing his father's knife, he scanned the thick undergrowth but saw nothing. Zuzu was as still as a startled deer, using all her senses to pinpoint the threat. Amber held her brother close, fearful of what new peril they faced.

A whisper of movement in the bush caused them to turn. From behind a tree emerged the Wolf.

The hunter had his bolt-action rifle shouldered and aimed at them.

"Are you lost, children?" he said quietly. "You're a long way from the lodge and heading in the wrong direction."

Connor felt deeply uneasy at the hunter's tone. He gripped his knife tighter, sensing he might have need of it. "No, we have a guide, thank you," he replied.

"That I see." The Wolf glanced at Zuzu, and then his pale

eyes flicked to Amber and Henri. "I thought you said your brother was dead."

"We rescued him," replied Amber curtly.

"Ah! Like I rescued you," said the Wolf, a pencil-thin smile on his lips. "And how did you repay me?" His expression hardened, the smile vanishing. "By sticking your nose into my business and injuring one of my men."

He swung the barrel of his rifle, aiming at Amber.

"You do realize there's a full-on battle raging up in that valley?" said Connor, hoping to divert his attention from her.

The Wolf nodded. "Your concern for my well-being is touching," he replied in a sarcastic tone. "But I have little problem avoiding the government troops, and Abel is smuggling the ivory out as we speak. You need to be more concerned about *your* future."

The Wolf kept his weapon trained on Amber.

"What are you going to do then? Shoot us all?" she challenged, her patience wearing thin.

A snarl of a grin spread across the Wolf's bearded face. "When a hunter has his prey in his sights, there's only *one* thing to do."

He curled his finger around the trigger. "Which of you wants to join my collection first?"

Connor instinctively stepped in front of Amber, shielding her with his body.

"Ahh! We have a volunteer," said the Wolf, closing one eye and lining up his sights.

Connor judged the distance too great for him to tackle the hunter before the gun went off. But he thought he might be able to distract or even injure the man by throwing his father's knife.

As he went to sling the blade, a dark shadow dropped silently from the bough above them.

The leopard landed full on the shoulders of the Wolf, knocking him to the ground. The rifle went off, tearing a hole in a nearby tree trunk. But the ambushing leopard wasn't frightened off by the blast. Instead the creature gave a ferocious growl and sank its fangs into the hunter's neck. The Wolf let out a strangled scream. He tried to fight off the beast, but the animal was too powerful for him.

As the leopard slowly suffocated the hunter, its green eyes glared at Connor and the others, daring them to approach. Connor, knife in hand, considered attempting a rescue but the leopard, pinning its victim beneath its razor claws, hissed a warning at his first tentative step. Then the animal bit down hard again and the Wolf fell still. As Connor cautiously backed away, the leopard dragged the limp, lifeless body of the hunter up into the tree.

46

The disheveled group of sister, brother, bodyguard and Batwa girl trekked slowly across the blisteringly hot savannah, keeping a clear distance from Dead Man's Hill as they made their way along the roundabout route to the lodge. Unnerved by the sheer brutality and savage swiftness of the leopard attack, their eyes constantly darted from bush to tree to scrub, alert for the slightest sign of danger.

"I think it's poetic justice," Amber declared as they passed safely through a thicket. "The hunter killed by the hunted."

Connor was inclined to agree. He held his father's knife close, having no intention of falling prey to the next predator they encountered—whether that be lion, hippo, hyena, snake or rebel soldier. "The Wolf deserved what was coming, that's for sure," he said. "But we must remember, he did help us in our time of need."

"I suppose so," said Amber reluctantly. "Of course, he then tried to kill us."

"Seems like everything in this country is trying to kill us!" remarked Henri with a weary laugh.

Connor was heartened to find Henri still had a sense of humor despite his recent ordeal. The boy limped ahead of him, the welts from his beating obviously causing him discomfort. And although Henri didn't complain, the sight of his suffering stirred up a tight knot of anger in Connor's belly. The cruelty inflicted by Blaze on a defenseless boy deserved retribution. And Connor hoped that the rebel had gotten his comeuppance at the hands of the government troops.

He wondered if the battle was over by now, with General Pascal either captured or dead. At the time, the fighting had been too chaotic to see who had the upper hand, but the government soldiers had secured the advantage of surprise, and it seemed highly unlikely the rebels would survive the attack.

Zuzu suddenly signed with the flat of her hand to get down. The four of them crouched behind a bush as an open-topped jeep crested the rise ahead. The vehicle drove hard and fast in their direction.

"Should we run?" suggested Henri, his voice tight with fear.

Connor shook his head. "They'll see us if we do."

The guttural roar of the diesel engine drew closer. Connor peered through a gap in the bush as the 4×4 skidded to a halt a stone's throw away from where they were hiding.

The driver stood up in his seat and scanned the terrain with his binoculars. "Damn it!" he swore.

"It's *Gunner*," hissed Amber in shocked delight.

Connor put a hand on her shoulder, preventing her from rising. She frowned in confusion. Connor shook his head and put a finger to his lips. After all they'd been through, he was wary of anyone they encountered in the park—especially an unexplained survivor of the ambush.

"Connor! Amber!" shouted the ranger, his tone urgent.

When no one appeared, Gunner shook his head in frustration and put the jeep into gear. At the very last second, Connor decided that answering the ranger was worth the risk. They were tired, hungry and hurting, and far from the lodge. They couldn't afford to miss a genuine chance of rescue. As Gunner was about to drive off, Connor stepped out from behind the bush and called to the ranger.

Gunner's craggy face broke into a relieved smile. "Connor! Thank God you're alive. I've been looking for you everywhere. Where are Amber and Henri?"

"How did you escape the ambush?" Connor questioned, his knife behind his back.

"By the skin of my teeth," Gunner replied, grinning. "I hid in an aardvark burrow. But it was a close call. Are Amber and Henri with you?"

Connor ignored the question and asked his own. "Why did you and Buju stop the safari convoy?"

Gunner's eyes narrowed at the surprise line of questioning. "Buju spotted a land mine. We were trying to establish if it was from the war or had been recently laid when the attack happened. Now tell me, are the Barbier children alive or not? Their parents are sick with worry."

Amber stood up with Henri in astonished disbelief. "They're *alive*?"

"Yes!" Gunner replied, hurriedly clambering out of the jeep to greet them, his glee turning to a mild look of surprise as Zuzu also emerged from behind the bush.

"But we saw their Land Rover crash and burn," said Connor, still cautious.

"I did too. So, while the rebels were slaughtering the presidential guard, I left my burrow and pulled them free." Gunner stared gravely at Amber and Henri, the siblings clasping hands. "I'll be honest; your parents weren't in good shape. But they could just about walk. It took us all night and most of the next day to reach the nearest medical center. The good news is they're recovering fast. But their major concern was for you two. I promised on my life to find you. And here you are!"

Turning to Connor, Gunner half raised his hands in surrender and smiled. "Now, Connor, are you going to put that knife of yours away or not? I have no wish to get stabbed trying to rescue you."

After a moment's deliberation, Connor decided to give

Gunner the benefit of the doubt, at least for now. He produced his father's knife from behind his back and sheathed it.

"I don't blame you for not trusting me," said Gunner, patting Connor on the shoulder. "Given the situation I don't trust anyone either. That's why I admitted the Barbiers to the medical center under a false name. Now let's get back to the lodge. Your friend too. This park is swarming with soldiers, and we don't want her mistaken for a rebel."

Amber explained the danger to Zuzu and, after some uncertainty on her part, managed to persuade her to climb into the jeep with them. The ranger gunned the engine and they shot off at high speed.

"Time is of the essence," said Gunner as he drove straight over some bushes. "I have a plane on standby to take us to the capital. There you'll be reunited with your parents."

47

Gunner drove up to the safari lodge's rarely used rear entrance, unlocked the gate, closed it behind them, then parked beside one of the guest suites.

"Why all the secrecy?" asked Connor as the ranger checked the grounds to make sure they were clear for them to proceed. "Surely the Burundian army is in control of the lodge, right?"

Gunner responded with a skeptical raise of an eyebrow. "Don't take anything for granted, Connor, especially in Africa. The Black Mamba has defeated forces five times his rebel group's size in the past. Besides, no one knows where you are or even that you're alive. I want to keep it that way until you're safely back with your respective parents. Now grab your essentials only—passport, travel documents, and a change of clothes—and leave the rest."

They moved from room to room, quickly gathering their most important belongings—except Amber, who stuffed a bag full of her best clothes and jewelry for Zuzu, fulfilling her promise. "I don't suppose we have time for a quick shower," she asked, tugging at her dirty, matted hair.

Gunner shook his head regretfully. "Sorry, can't risk it. That'll have to wait until later."

Next they entered the lodge's kitchen through the staff entrance. Some dislodged pans, a crumpled white hat and a pool of dried blood were the only remaining evidence of the chef's presence. Connor's alert level shot up, and he looked uneasily at the ranger.

"As I said, you can't take anything for granted," whispered Gunner as he raided the pantry. Then, peering through a small window in the kitchen's service door, he led them into the lounge.

The lavish room was deserted but appeared to have been the scene of some riotous celebration. The mirror behind the bar had been shattered. A spray of bullet holes peppered the main wall, several of the rounds having gone through the tribal shield, knocking the display askew. Connor also noticed that the zebra-skin rug on the hardwood floor was stained red—whether from blood or red wine it was impossible to tell, but there was an ominous dark trail leading from the bar out into the reception area.

"Do you think there's anyone still here?" asked Amber nervously.

"By the looks of it, we've missed the party," replied Gunner, plundering the bar for bottles of Coke and fresh water.

But Connor couldn't shake the feeling that they'd been led into a trap, one just waiting to be sprung. "So where's the army?"

Gunner shrugged. "Killing rebels in the park, I suppose. Now, you all look like you need refueling, and I don't want you dropping dead on me before we reach our final destination," he said, popping the tops of the drinks and handing them out. "Wait here while I call in the plane."

The ranger disappeared into the lodge's back office.

As the four of them guzzled down sugary Coke and greedily tucked into the chocolate bars, bananas and other snacks Gunner had gathered, Connor strode over to the bay windows overlooking the veranda and the plain beyond. Despite his fatigue, it was clear they weren't out of the danger zone yet and he needed to maintain a Code Orange level of alertness. Peering through the glass, he surveyed the lodge's grounds, keeping his eyes peeled for any sign of approaching rebels. There was no movement in the bush. In fact it looked almost too still. Then he spotted the body of a government soldier lying by the electric fence, half obscured in the grass. "Amber, we need to g—"

"My word, it's a miracle!" exclaimed a voice in accented English.

Connor spun around to see the bulging figure of Minister Feruzi standing in the doorway.

"I'd heard you'd escaped the ambush," said the minister for trade and tourism, smiling profusely and waddling over to the bar like a hippo heading for its watering hole. "But I never would have believed it until I saw you with my own eyes."

"Did you know one of your soldiers is lying dead out there?" said Connor, pointing to the electric fence at the lodge's boundary.

"Oh yes! Minister Rawasa has returned to the capital, and I've been left here to pick up the pieces," he replied with a what-can-you-do shrug. "But, joy of joys, we have good news at last! You're all safe and sound."

His gaze fell upon Zuzu standing with them at the bar, his nose turning up slightly at her presence. "And who's this?"

"Our guide," replied Amber with enthusiasm. "She's been a lifeline for us."

"I'm sure she has. Burundians are a most hospitable people," said the minister assuredly. "But now it's *my* responsibility to look after you."

He wrapped his chubby arms around Amber's and Henri's shoulders, Amber looking distinctly uncomfortable and Henri wincing beneath the man's sweaty touch. Only then did the minister notice the red welts covering Henri's body, and he let go. "Oh, my poor boy, what have they done to you?"

The ranger strode back in. "Plane's on its way. Let's make a—" He stopped and stared at the minister.

"Gunner?" exclaimed Minister Feruzi, staring back in equal amazement. "My God, another risen from the ashes! Are there any more of you?"

With a solemn, stern shake of his head, the ranger replied, "I found Buju, or what was left of him."

"That's tragic to hear," said the minister. "But have you any news of Laurent or Cerise? We have reason to believe they may have escaped the ambush too."

"I wouldn't know," replied Gunner as he beckoned Connor and the others to join him. "Time to go, kids."

"What's the rush, Gunner?" Minister Feruzi demanded, his pudgy eyes narrowing in suspicion. "This lodge is now secure."

"Are you sure about that, Minister?" questioned the ranger with a sharp jerk of his head at Connor, Amber, Henri and Zuzu, urging them to hurry.

"Children, you *mustn't* go with him," insisted Minister Feruzi. "This man's a prime suspect in the ambush."

Connor and the others froze halfway between the two men. *So I was right to be suspicious of the ranger?*

"Don't believe him," said Gunner. "He's the one behind all this. *He* chose the route for the sunset safari, even though there's a far better place closer to the lodge."

Minister Feruzi laughed. "That's ridiculous! Think about it, children: who stopped the convoy in the middle of that riverbed?"

"That's only because Buju spotted a mine!" argued Gunner. "Otherwise we'd have all been blown to pieces. Connor, why do you think Minister Feruzi was so far back in the convoy? His vehicle escaped unharmed because he *knew* the ambush was going to happen."

Caught between the ranger and the minister, Connor wondered whom to believe. One of them was lying. Amber and the others looked to him to make the decision.

"We have to go *now!*" insisted Gunner, his eyes darting from the door to the veranda.

"Given the situation, I don't trust anyone," said Connor, repeating the ranger's words back at him.

For Connor, Gunner's story of his escape had always seemed too good to be true. He also thought it unlikely that a government minister would be in league with a rebel military group. He made a move toward Minister Feruzi, the man opening his arms to receive them. Then Connor remembered the dead body of the soldier by the wire. The minister had said the lodge was secure, but how could that be if the guards were dead?

At the last moment Connor changed his mind, nodding to Amber and the others to go with Gunner instead.

"I can't save you now, children," said Minister Feruzi as General Pascal strode into the lounge, accompanied by Blaze, No Mercy and half a dozen rebel soldiers.

48

"I see you found my strays," remarked General Pascal, heading straight for the bar as if he owned it. His eyes bloodshot, his skin oily with sweat and his injured arm wrapped in a bandage, the rebel leader looked the worse for wear following his battle against the government troops. But the infamous military skill of the man had evidently secured him another victory.

"Drink!" he barked to one of his soldiers. Scurrying behind the bar, the boy grabbed a bottle and filled an empty glass. The general drained it in one hit and the boy replenished it immediately.

"I was told that the army had been diverted to sector *four* of the park!" growled General Pascal, glaring at the minister. "So how come soldiers attacked our camp this morning in sector *eight*?"

Minister Feruzi blanched at the news. "Th-the major general must have changed his plans without informing me."

General Pascal stabbed a finger at the minister. "You realize I lost good warriors," he snapped. "What's worse, the army's probably blown half the diamonds to dust!"

Tugging a handkerchief from his shirt pocket, the minister mopped his brow in panic. "I assure you, the major general was instructed to search the southern sector of the park. But what about the diamonds? Do you still have control? Are there *any* left?"

"Don't worry your fat face about it! My forces still command the valley and there'll be enough for everyone," replied the general, grimacing as he inspected his swollen arm. "First let's deal with this little problem of my strays. Then we can discuss the future of this country, and your place in it."

Stepping forward, Gunner spat at the minister's feet. "You treacherous piece of scum—you traded our lives for diamonds!"

Minister Feruzi glanced down at the spit smearing his shoe. "You shouldn't have done that, Gunner."

General Pascal nodded a silent order to No Mercy. A deafening *bang* rang in all their ears as the boy soldier shot Gunner in the chest.

"Consider yourself fired," said Minister Feruzi with a gloating smirk as the ranger writhed and groaned in pain on the floor.

"No, Gunner, no!" cried Amber, dropping down beside

the ranger and pressing her hands to his wound, blood ooz-
ing from between her fingers. Connor kept Henri close as
Zuzu stared in wide-eyed shock at the boy soldier standing
over the ranger.

"Finish him off," said the general, his tone bored. "I can't
stand the groaning."

On a do-or-die impulse, Connor snatched one of the
tribal spears from the wall. "Stay back!" he warned.

General Pascal eyed the old weapon with amusement as
he leaned against the bar. "Now what are you going to do
with that, my White Warrior?" he inquired. "Spear a lion?"

"No," Connor replied, pointing the iron tip at him. "Skewer
a snake!"

The Black Mamba laughed. "You have fighting spirit, I
grant you that. But playtime's over. Drop the spear or Blaze
kills your girl."

Blaze drew a handgun and aimed it at Amber's head.
Connor turned the spear on the rebel. If he was quick, he
could perhaps drive it through the man's chest before he
pulled the trigger. But No Mercy would have more than
enough time to shoot Gunner again. And then what? Connor
glanced toward the double glass doors. He wondered if they
could flee via the veranda. Then a rebel soldier appeared on
the other side of the bay windows, cutting off their escape
route. Left with no option, Connor discarded the spear, the
weapon clattering to the wooden floor.

"You disappoint me," said General Pascal, coughing into his fist. "I'd hoped you would die fighting like a warrior."

The general headed for the main door, beckoning Minister Feruzi and the half dozen rebel soldiers to accompany him.

"Blaze, kill the strays," he ordered. "Any way you wish. Just make sure the Batwa girl, who put the arrow through my arm, suffers most."

49

Forced at gunpoint to kneel, Connor, Henri and Zuzu joined
Amber on the floor slick with Gunner's blood. The ranger's
breathing was now labored and rasping. He'd fallen unconscious with the pain but was clinging to life. Connor's mind
was racing, trying desperately to think of some way out of
their predicament. But No Mercy kept his AK-47 trained on
them, and Connor knew that at the first sign of resistance
he'd simply shoot them dead.

Blaze unsheathed his machete and caressed the razor-
edged blade with a finger. "This is my weapon of choice," he
said with a sadistic grin. "I can cut, cleave, slice, hack, chop or
behead you with one stroke of this beauty."

The rebel paced slowly in front of them, drawing out the
tension as he casually swung the blade.

He jutted his chin at Zuzu. "I'll leave you for last, Batwa," he spat with contempt. "Then you can know of the suffering that awaits you."

Understanding the threat but not the words, Zuzu shrank away, but her eyes remained fixated on No Mercy.

Blaze prodded the tip of his machete into Henri's chest. "You, I'll skin like a rabbit. Hang your hide out to dry in the hot sun."

Confronted by his tormentor once more, Henri began to sob and tremble uncontrollably.

Blaze laughed. "Pathetic!"

Leaving the boy quivering at the thought of his impending gruesome demise, Blaze crouched before Amber. He pushed aside a lock of her hair with his machete, then rattled his macabre necklace in front of her face.

"Perhaps I'll add one of your teeth to my necklace," he said, leering at her.

"I hope you burn in hell," she said, her eyes fierce and defiant.

Blaze blew her a mocking kiss. "And I hope I meet you there."

Connor shook with fury. Powerless to do anything, he could only watch as Blaze tormented each of them in turn. Grimly aware that it was now a stark matter of life and death, Connor resolved to die trying to save Amber and Henri. He still had his father's knife tucked on his hip. He wondered if Zuzu was thinking the same thing. She hadn't taken her eyes off the boy soldier and his gun. Perhaps if he made a move to tackle Blaze, she'd go for No Mercy and try to wrestle the weapon from him.

The rebel regarded Connor. "I know what you're thinking, but if I see you even twitch, I promise to make your girl *truly* suffer."

Connor glared up at Blaze. "I'll tear you limb from limb if you dare lay a finger on Amber or Henri."

Blaze smirked. "It's me who's going to enjoy taking *you* apart, piece by piece. But who should go first? Eeny, meeny, miney, moe," he said in a singsong voice, the tip of the blade swinging from Connor to Amber to Henri and back again. "Catch a lion by the nose. If he roars, let him go. Eeny, meeny, miney, *moe*."

The machete came to a stop in front of Connor. Blaze grinned. With a violent sweep of the blade, he cleared one of the lounge's coffee tables, scattering the candles and place mats onto the floor. Then he grabbed Connor by the hair and held the blade to his throat.

"So, what will it be—long or short sleeves?"

Connor stared up at him, at once baffled and petrified by the question.

"No Mercy, hold out his arm," Blaze ordered.

Suddenly it dawned on Connor what the rebel had in

mind. He struggled wildly, but Blaze pressed the machete harder into his neck, drawing a thin line of blood.

"Don't fret. It only hurts *after* I cut your arm off," explained Blaze as No Mercy slung his AK-47 over his shoulder and seized Connor's wrist. With surprising strength, he pinned Connor's arm down on the coffee table.

"*Deo?*" uttered Zuzu, staring at No Mercy.

The boy soldier didn't react.

"*Deo! C'est ta sœur!*"

No Mercy looked at her uncomprehendingly.

Zuzu became more frantic. "*Deo! Mon frère! S'il te plaît, ne lui fais pas de mal! Je t'en prie.*"

"*Tais-toi!*" barked Blaze, striking her with the back of his hand.

The blow was so violent that Zuzu was flung against the bar, her head cracking against the mahogany panel.

No Mercy frowned, still holding Connor's arm, but his attention was now on Zuzu. Her lip bleeding, tears rolling down her cheeks, she continued to beg the boy soldier to listen to her. Connor couldn't understand a word. His heart thudded in his chest as the blood rushed through his ears. A paralyzing wave of panic overwhelmed him, and his limbs refused to respond as Blaze took up position to hack off his right arm.

"Don't close your eyes. You need to see this," said Blaze,

licking his lips in anticipation. "I promise you'll remember this for the rest of your life."

The machete came slicing down toward its target.

Amber screamed and Henri covered his eyes. Zuzu's shouting grew louder. Connor fought to break his paralysis, scrabbling for his knife. At the last second No Mercy let go of his wrist and Connor snatched back his arm, the blade embedding itself deep into the wooden table.

Blaze glared in furious outrage at No Mercy. "You idiot! Why did you let go?" he roared.

As he tried to yank the machete out of the table, No Mercy picked up the discarded spear. Before Blaze knew what was happening, the boy soldier had buried the iron tip deep in his back. Blaze let out an agonized howl as the spear pierced his heart and burst out through his rib cage.

No Mercy twisted the shaft one last time and Blaze slumped to the floor. "That's for making me believe my family were all dead!"

50

Still trembling from shock, his arm clutched protectively to him, Connor watched in stunned amazement as Zuzu rushed over and embraced her long-lost brother. No Mercy stood rigid and emotionless, unsure how to handle such affection, his first in years. Then he surrendered himself to his sister, resting his head against hers.

Amber, clasping her own brother, smiled with joy at the heaven-sent reunion. His eyes red and puffy, Henri stared at the contorted body of Blaze, the spear tip protruding from his chest. "Is he dead?"

No Mercy nodded.

"Good," said Henri, free at last of his tormentor.

Connor snapped back to his senses. Blaze might be dead, but there were at least half a dozen more rebels led by the Black Mamba who weren't. Getting to his feet, Connor rushed over to Gunner. The ranger was still breathing.

Judging that the boy soldier was now on their side, Connor said, "No Mercy, help me."

"My name is Deo," said the boy soldier softly. "That's my *real* name."

"Well, Deo, I'm Connor, and I need your help to carry the man you shot."

Zuzu let her brother go, and between them they lifted the ranger off the floor. Gunner regained consciousness with a gasp of pain. Manhandling him out of the lounge, they staggered into the kitchen. Halfway across, straining under his dead weight, they were forced to put him down and rest a moment.

"Leave . . . me," moaned Gunner.

"No," said Connor, putting the ranger's arm over his shoulder to try again. "You came back for us. We're taking you with us."

Gunner grimaced. "I . . . won't . . . make it."

"Yes, you will," said Amber firmly, grabbing a first-aid kit from a shelf. Riffling through the box, she pulled out a dressing and bandage and worked fast to stanch the bleeding.

"Hurry," urged Henri, peering back into the lounge. "I can hear someone coming."

Amber wrapped the bandage several times around Gunner's chest, then tied it off. Connor and Deo picked up the ranger and lurched toward the staff exit. Zuzu opened the door, first making sure the way was clear before giving them the signal to follow and hurrying out into the bright sunshine. Using as much natural cover as they could to stay out of sight, they stumbled from building to building. Deo warned them that the main gate was guarded by rebel soldiers. More were congregated beside a bunch of jeeps parked outside the lodge. Henri even spotted two boy soldiers with their feet dangling in the private pool of one of the guest suites.

Panting heavily from the exertion of carrying the ranger, Connor and Deo eventually reached Gunner's jeep. Between them, they lifted him into the rear passenger seat. Amber clambered in beside him, keeping the ranger upright. The others crammed themselves into any remaining space. Connor jumped into the driver's seat and turned the key in the ignition. The engine kicked into life, sounding ferociously loud amid the silence.

"Here goes nothing," he said, engaging first gear and shooting off with a spin of the tires.

As he headed for the lodge's rear entrance, there was a shout. One of the rebels in the pool had heard the jeep start and raised the alarm. Gunfire raked the ground on either side of the vehicle, some of the bullets ricocheting off the jeep's metalwork. Ducking down, Connor floored the accelerator and drove straight at the closed gates. With a tremendous crash, the metal gates flew apart as the jeep careered on through. Hurtling on at high speed, the vehicle thumped and bumped along the dirt track as Connor zigzagged their way down the ridge toward the savannah plain.

"They're following us!" cried Amber, who was desperately trying to keep pressure on Gunner's chest wound.

Connor glanced in the rearview mirror and saw a convoy of rebel jeeps racing after them.

"There's the plane!" shouted Henri, pointing to a private jet making its approach toward the airstrip in the distance.

As they reached the base of the ridge, Connor checked his mirror again. The rebels were close on their tail and gaining fast. If they made it to the plane at all, Connor knew they'd be cutting it dangerously close. He tried to recall the route their driver had taken on their arrival, but there was no obvious road in sight. So he decided to head directly for the airstrip.

"Hang on!" he warned. "This could get a little hairy."

His passengers clinging on for dear life, Connor drove even faster, weaving between rocks and bushes. The rutted terrain punished the jeep's suspension, threatening to shake the vehicle to pieces. Behind, the sound of gunfire pursued them, several bullets finding their mark in the rear panel, but Connor didn't dare look back again for fear of colliding with a half-buried rock or dropping into a hidden gully.

Less than a mile away now, the jet plane had landed and was turning around at the end of the runway in preparation for takeoff. More bullets whizzed past. The jeep's windshield shattered, and glass showered down on Connor and the others. Deo swiveled around in his seat, shouldered his AK-47 and returned fire, trying to slow their pursuers down.

They hit the runway at speed, Connor almost rolling their vehicle as he spun the wheel and headed toward salvation. He skidded to a halt beside the jet, its engines still turning over. The pilot lowered the automatic stairs, urging them from his cockpit to hurry.

Scrambling out of the jeep, Connor yanked open the passenger door and helped drag Gunner out. They had almost reached the steps when four rebel jeeps surrounded them.

51

As the dust settled, the Black Mamba stepped out of his vehicle.

"I gravely underestimated you, my White Warrior," he declared, his tone bitter yet admiring. "I don't know what training you've had, but you're certainly no ordinary boy."

With the barrels of a dozen AK-47s pointed at their heads, Connor and the others lowered the ranger to the ground. They'd been so close to making it out alive. In a final act of protection, Connor shielded Amber and Henri behind him and waited for the rebel leader to give the order to open fire.

General Pascal turned his bloodshot eyes upon Deo. "Of all my boy warriors, you were the *last* I expected to betray me. After all I've done for you. I made you into a man. A great warrior!" The general shook his head in dark disappointment. "But I am a forgiving commander. Return to your rightful family and I'll let you live."

Like a benevolent father, the general opened his arms

wide to welcome him back to the fold. Deo glanced at Zuzu, his sister looking up at him with eyes pleading for him to stay.

"Make your decision," said General Pascal impatiently. "On which side do you stand, No Mercy? Life or death?"

Drawing his sister close, Deo removed his red beret and tossed it at the general's feet. "Zuzu's my *real* family," he replied. "I'd rather die in love than live in hate."

"Oh well," said the general, raising his Glock 17 and taking aim. "It saddens me to have to execute you, but—"

General Pascal spluttered and choked, his hand going to his heart. Suddenly he collapsed to the dirt, his eyes bulging and his body contorting. Connor glimpsed the general's swollen-veined arm and recalled what Zuzu had said about her arrow tips. *Toxique.* The lethal poison had worked its way through the general's system and was now attacking his heart.

In the resulting confusion, as his soldiers rushed to his aid, Connor and the others dragged Gunner up the steps and into the plane. Before any rebel had even noticed, the pilot was raising the automatic stairs and rolling for takeoff. The blast from the jet engines sent up billowing clouds of red dust, blinding the rebels. By the time the air cleared and they started to fire off rounds, the plane was already halfway down the runway and gathering speed to takeoff velocity.

Connor and the others buckled themselves into their

seats as the jet lifted off the ground and soared into the air. And with it soared everyone's hearts. Against all the odds, they had escaped. No one could stop them now.

As the pilot banked the plane toward the country's capital, Connor caught a glimpse through the window of the Burundian army, a full contingent of reinforcements closing in from all directions of the park. Confronted by an overwhelming force, the rebels were either fleeing in panic or laying down their weapons in surrender.

Lying back in the impossibly plush leather seat of the private jet, Zuzu muttered something to her brother and he nodded in agreement.

"What did she say?" asked Connor.

Amber looked over, a relieved smile on her face as she held Henri tight, having just told him that she loved him.

"Cut the head off the snake and the body dies."

52

"The Black Mamba poisoned! How apt," remarked Major General Tabu Baratuza with a deep rumbling laugh, his French translated a second later in Connor's new earpiece. "Let it not be said that justice isn't served in Africa."

There was a ripple of appreciative laughter among the guests assembled in the Burundian presidential palace's ornate ballroom. The expansive hall was brimming with politicians, foreign dignitaries, well-to-do businessmen and their accompanying wives, all gathered to celebrate the inauguration of Adrien Rawasa, the former minister for energy and mines, as the new president of Burundi.

"So what's Michel Feruzi's punishment going to be?" asked Gaspard Sibomana, the newly appointed minister for trade and tourism. "Death by eating?"

The guests laughed heartily.

Ambassador Laurent Barbier and his family did not. Less

than a week since their escape, the ambush and its fallout was still too raw for them.

"How can they joke about such things?" said Cerise bitterly. Whereas her husband appeared relatively unscathed as a result of the car crash, Cerise now bore a slight limp and still wore dressings on her arms where she'd been badly burned in the vehicle fire.

"Death is all too familiar in Africa," explained Colonel Black. "If they don't laugh about it, the only other option is to cry. And that's not in the nature of these people."

"But who'd have believed Feruzi was a traitor?" said Laurent with a sorrowful shake of his head. "After the wonderful work we'd accomplished together on the park, I considered him one of my friends. All I can say is that I'm very glad I hired your services, Colonel. If it weren't for Connor here, we'd be mourning today, not celebrating."

"I expected nothing less of him," declared Colonel Black, glancing at Connor. "He's his father's son to the core."

For Connor that was high commendation indeed, and he felt a swell of pride at being compared to his father. Colonel Black didn't need to say any more to express his deep regard for Connor's accomplishments. The colonel was a man of action, not words. He'd been the first to board the plane when they'd landed in Bujumbura to check on Connor, before organizing the group's swift transfer to a private health clinic for immediate medical treatment. And while Connor was being treated for his wounds and recuperating in the days that followed, the colonel had been a constant presence on the ward.

Cerise leaned forward and kissed Connor lightly on both cheeks. *"Merci, merci,"* she said. "You kept our children safe. You'll always be welcome at our home in Paris, Connor."

"Thank you, Mrs. Barbier, that's very kind of you," he replied. "After all we've been through together, Henri, Amber and I have certainly become close friends."

Henri stood by his mother's side, the red welts across his arms and body mostly faded; although Connor suspected the memory of his beating would leave a mental scar. Henri smiled shyly up at Connor, then hugged him hard around the waist. "Can't you protect us forever?"

Connor ruffled his hair. "You're going home, Henri. No one's going to hurt you there."

"But I'm still scared," he admitted quietly. Then he rummaged in his pocket. "I almost forgot. Your watch."

He passed Connor the Rangeman, still barely a scratch on its face.

"No, it's yours," said Connor, pushing it back into his hand, realizing the boy needed his birthday gift more than he did. "Any time you feel scared, just put it on."

Henri gratefully clasped his gift. "I will," he said.

Amber stepped forward and took Connor's hand. She stared at him a moment, her green eyes as striking as ever but now more wary and world-wise since her ordeal with the rebels. Her lustrous red hair brushed against his face as she kissed him warmly on both cheeks, lingering a little longer than necessary. She clearly wanted to express her true feelings for him but felt restricted by the presence of her parents. "You'll always have a place in my heart," she whispered, squeezing his hand one last time before letting go.

As Laurent and his family were called away to meet with a contingent of reporters, Connor and Colonel Black hung back, keeping a low profile. Then a wheelchair rolled unexpectedly into the ballroom and Connor stared in astonishment.

"Gunner!" he exclaimed, hurrying over. "I didn't think we'd see you out of the hospital so soon."

"In Africa only the strong survive," replied the ranger, his chest heavily bandaged and his voice even more gravelly than before. "And *you* are definitely a lion."

Connor was honored by such a comparison. "What does that make you, then?"

"At the moment, a sloth!" He winked at the young nurse pushing his wheelchair. "But I'll soon be back on my feet."

"Joseph Gunner, I assume?" said Colonel Black, striding over to introduce himself. "Colonel Douglas Black, Connor's . . . guardian. You were unconscious when we first met, but I want to thank you for helping rescue him and the Barbier family."

Gunner laughed, then winced in pain. "It was Connor who saved *me* in the end! You have a remarkable boy there."

"Yes, I know," replied the colonel. "In fact I want to talk to you about that. Connor's spoken well of you, and I have a proposition you may be interested in."

"Well, I'm all ears, Colonel," replied Gunner. "In my current state I'm not exactly inundated with work."

"If you'll excuse us, Connor," said the colonel, inviting the ranger to join him in a side chamber off the ballroom. "Gunner, I'm looking for a man I can trust to teach survival skills to some other young guardians of mine."

"Sounds interesting. Tell me more . . ."

As Colonel Black pushed the ranger's wheelchair toward the room to discuss his proposal in private, Gunner looked back over his shoulder and called to Connor. "Just remember: it doesn't matter whether you are a lion or a gazelle; when the sun comes up, you'd better be running."

Connor laughed. He'd had quite enough of running for a while and was looking forward to the relatively quiet life of overseeing an operation from the safety of Guardian HQ. He helped himself to a fancy chicken skewer from a passing waiter and was wondering where Amber was when a finger gently tapped him on the shoulder. He turned around to find himself face-to-face with the new Burundian president.

"I just wished to personally express my appreciation for ensuring the safe return of the Barbier children," said President

Rawasa, his tone surprisingly soft and delicate for a man now in charge of a whole country. "It would have been a tragic outcome with serious international repercussions for our nation if they had not survived. In fact, I don't know how you made it out of that valley alive."

"We were very fortunate," replied Connor, "and were helped by Zuzu, the girl from a local Batwa tribe."

"Yes," he said thoughtfully. "I must not forget her either."

As President Rawasa lightly shook his hand, Connor caught a strong scent of fine French musk cologne emanating from the president. The distinctive smell instantly transported Connor back to the hidden valley and the mysterious stranger who'd stood just beyond the light of the kerosene lamps. Connor had assumed it had been the white man from the burning tanker. But he'd smelled the exact same aroma the first time he'd been introduced to Adrien Rawasa at the safari lodge. And how many other men in this country wore such an expensive and particular cologne?

"Anything wrong?" asked President Rawasa with an inquiring smile.

Connor shook his head. "No, not at all. I just remembered I have to tell the colonel something."

53

Forcing himself to walk slowly so as not to arouse the president's suspicion, Connor headed for the side chamber to speak with the colonel. Finding the room empty, he passed through a set of double doors leading to a long hallway. The corridor was deserted, but Connor could hear voices in a room farther down. Quickly and quietly, he hurried along the polished wooden floor, the sounds of revelry fading behind him with every step.

As he approached the door to the room, he noticed it was slightly ajar and through the gap saw Laurent Barbier. Connor judged the diplomat needed to know about his suspicions just as much as the colonel. He was about to knock on the door and go in when he spied the man Laurent was talking to and froze in his tracks.

The ghost from his past had materialized once more.

The ashen-faced stranger stood opposite the diplomat.

Unremarkable in height or appearance, he nonetheless exuded a sinister and baleful presence that seemed to contaminate the room like a virus. Just looking at him made Connor's skin crawl as if he were covered with driver ants all over again. Connor flattened himself against the wall and, with a growing disquiet, eavesdropped on their conversation.

"You never told me my children would be in danger!" snapped Laurent.

"Such risks go with the territory," replied the man, indifferent to Mr. Barbier's fury.

"But why wasn't I informed about the ambush in advance? We could all have been killed!"

The man replied with a barely perceptible shrug of the shoulders. "Sometimes, the less you know, the better. You hired protection—of an unorthodox sort, granted—so your children are alive. Besides, you're going to be one very rich man."

"Mr. Gray, when it comes to life, there's *nothing* more important than family."

"Ah, yes," he replied with a scornful smirk. "So that's why you had an affair?"

The diplomat was embarrassed into silence.

Mr. Gray evidently enjoyed putting the man to shame as he pressed the point. "Now, you don't want Mrs. Barbier knowing about your other little liaisons, do you?" His eyes flicked toward the door, and Connor sharply pulled back.

His breath catching in his throat, Connor prayed the ghost hadn't spotted him.

"So let's proceed with our business," continued Mr. Gray, returning his attention to Mr. Barbier. "Tell me, is the new president fully on board?"

"Yes," replied Laurent tersely. "The Ruvubu National Park will be a park in name only. We'll keep up the appearance of a functioning safari destination, but there'll be no tourists. The park's to be closed off for diamond mining."

"Excellent. And Equilibrium has the sole mining concession?"

"In return for keeping President Rawasa in office . . . by whatever means necessary."

Mr. Gray nodded. "And you, Ambassador, will smuggle the diamonds out, using your diplomatic immunity from customs clearance, and ensure they're properly certified."

"Yes," replied Laurent. "That is the agreement."

Mr. Gray produced a small suede bag full to the brim with uncut diamonds and handed it to the diplomat. Laurent went over to a table upon which lay a black leather diplomatic briefcase. He unlocked it and deposited the bag inside a hidden compartment.

"Now that our business is concluded, Ambassador," said Mr. Gray, heading out a side door, "you can enjoy the party. After all, you've just become a multimillionaire."

54

Connor darted across the hallway and into the opposite room just as Laurent Barbier emerged, carrying his briefcase. Reeling from the shock of Mr. Barbier's corrupt dealings, it dawned on Connor that he was amid a nest of vipers. With their lives in potentially grave danger, the colonel was the *only* man he could trust. Connor had to find him, and fast.

"You crop up in all the wrong places and at all the wrong times, Connor Reeves."

Connor spun to find Mr. Gray directly behind him.

"Yes, I know who you are," he said, relishing the wide-eyed look of horrified surprise on Connor's face.

As desperate as Connor was to escape the room, his feet were rooted to the spot. Up close Mr. Gray was an unnerving sight. His lean face was plain and ordinary—but it was that dull ordinariness that made him terrifying, like a waxwork come to life. His skin was dry and anemic, his ice-gray eyes devoid of all human warmth. And his breath, as he moved closer to Connor, possessed the dank smell of a tomb.

"So, Connor, what do *you* know?" he asked, almost as casually as if he were chatting about the weather. But the underlying menace was still there.

"I know your name, but not who you are," replied Connor, his mouth going dry with fear.

"I'm afraid that's *more* than enough." Mr. Gray let out a sigh, then went silent as if contemplating Connor's fate.

"I saw you on that tanker in Somalia," said Connor, finding his tongue again. "What were you doing there? Why did you shoot that pirate? Are you an assassin?"

Mr. Gray narrowed his eyes at him. "Young boys have such inquiring minds. So many questions. But you know what they say?" He paused for effect. "Curiosity killed the cat."

Connor wanted to run for his life. But his legs failed to respond. A good thing, perhaps, since he sensed that the merest attempt to flee would prompt Mr. Gray to eliminate him in the blink of an eye. Now, instead of surrendering to his fear, Connor became defiant.

"Well, if you intend to kill me, you'd better not miss this time," he said.

"I *never* miss," snapped Mr. Gray, evidently offended at such a slur on his marksmanship.

"You did at the mine."

Mr. Gray answered with a thin dour smile. "I shot exactly who I meant to."

Connor frowned. "The rebel soldier?"

Mr. Gray nodded once.

"You were *helping* me to escape?" said Connor, incredulous at such a notion.

"I wouldn't call it help exactly. Just balancing the odds. Equilibrium, one might call it."

"What is this Equilibrium?" demanded Connor. "You mentioned it before."

Mr. Gray tutted. "Remember the cat! On that point, neutralizing you here and now would raise too many awkward questions." He leaned forward, ensuring he had Connor's full attention. "This is our second encounter, Connor Reeves. Pray that we don't have a third."

Connor swallowed uneasily. "So what are you going to do to me?"

Mr. Gray leaned in even closer, his pale face filling Connor's vision. Connor found himself mesmerized by the man's fathomless eyes. He seemed to be plunging into their icy depths, drawn down deeper and deeper like a drowning man. At the same time, Mr. Gray whispered words like drops of poison in his ear, his hushed, almost breathless voice worming its way deep into Connor's subconscious. *"Forget my face . . . I never existed . . . You never heard my name . . . Equilibrium means nothing . . . I am just a ghost to you . . ."*

55

"There you are! I was beginning to think you'd left without saying good-bye."

Connor blinked, shaking his head as if he'd been woken from a trance.

"What are you doing in here all alone?" asked Amber as she entered the room.

Connor looked around, somewhat bewildered. He found himself in a little-used office with an old wooden chair, a desk and an out-of-date calendar on the wall. The last thing he could recall was helping himself to a chicken skewer from a passing waiter in the ballroom. Wondering how on earth he'd ended up here, a vague recollection surfaced in his foggy mind. "Um, looking for Colonel Black, I think."

Connor knew there was something very important he had to tell the colonel. It was on the tip of his tongue, but for the life of him he couldn't remember.

"Well, he's in the main ballroom," said Amber. "And did you know Gunner's here? That man must be as strong as a lion to recover so fast." Noticing the dazed look on Connor's face, she asked, "Are you all right?"

Connor nodded. "Yes, fine. A little tired, that's all."

"I'm not surprised," said Amber kindly as she stepped closer to him, a joyful smile on her lips. "By the way, I have some great news."

"What is it?"

"My father just came out of a meeting." Again something stirred in Connor's memory like an itch he couldn't scratch. "He organized a French aid fund to sponsor Zuzu and Deo. They're going to be given a proper home, an education, an income. A chance to live their own lives."

"That's wonderful," said Connor, the good news clearing his sluggish mind. "We should go and congratulate them."

"Hold on a minute," said Amber, grabbing his hand and pulling him back. She gently closed the door to the room. "Before we return to the party, we have some unfinished business."

"We do?" said Connor, trying to jog his memory again.

"This time there are no snakes, ants, crocodiles or leopards to disturb us . . ." Without warning, she kissed him full on the lips.

Connor's breath was taken away. He wrapped his arms

round her and kissed her back. The horrors of their recent ordeal seemed to shrink to nothing in their passionate embrace. In the back of his mind, though, a voice was telling him to stop. The Guardian organization had laid down specific rules.

But, hey, if I hadn't taken a few risks in my life, I probably wouldn't be around to enjoy this one . . .

Yet in his heart of hearts he knew what was *really* wrong about kissing Amber. The revelation caused Connor to pull away.

"Don't stop," she murmured, her eyes half closed and dreamy.

"I'm sorry. But I must. I'm supposed to be your bodyguard."

"And you're making me feel safe. Very safe." She leaned in for another kiss.

Connor gently held her at bay. "I can't be your boyfriend. I made an oath not to get involved with clients. When I commit to something, I don't break that commitment."

Amber studied him intently with a mixture of longing and bittersweet admiration. "You're the first boy I've met who actually does what he says and stands by his word." She seemed about to cry. "I respect you for that."

Stepping away, she straightened her hair and regained her composure. Her green eyes glistened, but her expression remained strong and self-assured.

"When you're ready for another commitment, Connor, give me a call. But I won't wait forever."

Amber kissed him briefly on both cheeks, then opened the door and headed out of the room. Connor's last glimpse of her was a flash of flame-red hair disappearing down the hallway.

56

"How's Operation Hawk-Eye going?" asked Connor, happy to be back in the comms seat in Alpha team's briefing room.

"Well, there've been no more eggs!" Amir replied, the monitor revealing a more confident expression on his friend's face compared to the last time they'd spoken, when he'd failed to react after a protestor had slung an egg at his Principal. "But there was a bomb."

"A bomb!" Connor exclaimed. "Are you all right? What happened?"

Amir nodded. "Thanks to your advice I spotted it early." He waved a pair of sunglasses in front of the camera. "You reminded me that the mind is the best weapon. So, using my IT skills, I upgraded the lenses to detect sudden movements. My early-warning system helped me save my Principal by leaping in front of him as the bomb was thrown."

"How on earth did you survive?"

"It was a *water* bomb," explained Amir, laughing at Connor's wide-eyed look of shock. "I got soaked!"

Connor laughed too. "Well, I'm pleased you're in such high spirits. I'm just sorry I wasn't around the last couple of weeks, but I've been a little tied up."

"Don't worry about it," said Amir. "Charley's been my support, and I know you were gunning for me too." He moved closer to the screen and squinted. "I see you lost your watch. That thing was indestructible! Is there nothing you can't lose or break on an assignment?"

Connor felt his face flush at being found out. He'd replaced the watch he'd given Henri with a brand-new Rangeman at airport duty-free on the way home. "How do you know?" he asked.

Amir rolled his eyes. "That's the series three edition. It's the newest model. You can tell by the red accents on the dial. Yours was a series two."

"Well, whatever series, your gift was a godsend," said Connor with a rueful smile. "I'd have literally been lost without it."

"So how was Africa?" asked Amir.

Connor hesitated before replying. "It's the most beautiful, awe-inspiring and . . . lethal place on Earth. Africa just gets under your skin. Despite everything that happened, I'd go back in a heartbeat. Although I might not take a safari anytime soon!"

"Sounds to me like you need a *real* vacation," said Amir.

Connor nodded in agreement. "When you're back, let's ask the colonel for some time off."

"Great idea! A guardian break!" There was a voice in the background and Amir glanced offscreen. "Sorry, Connor, I've got to go. Duty calls."

"I understand. Stay safe, Amir. Alpha Control, signing off."

As Connor closed down the video app, a clawed hand suddenly grabbed his left shoulder and he half jumped, half winced.

"Hey, pussycat!" said Ling, baring her teeth in a mock snarl. "When will you be ready for our final deciding match?"

"Not for a good few weeks," he replied, loosening up his stiff shoulder. "The doctor says I need to rest; otherwise I'll rip my stitches again."

Ling tutted in disappointment. "Excuses, excuses," she said. "I suppose we could play tic-tac-toe with your scars while we wait."

"You need to let him rest, Ling," said Charley, glancing over as she typed up the team's daily occurrence log. "He's still in recovery."

"Why does Connor get all your sympathy?" Marc questioned, raising his own shirt to reveal a small scar across his belly. "I had my appendix taken out in an emergency operation!"

"Shame they didn't take your voice box out at the same

time," said Jason. "Then we wouldn't have to listen to all your complaining."

"It's nothing to joke about," protested Marc. "I almost *died*."

Connor said nothing, but he thought he'd prefer acute appendicitis to fighting rebel soldiers and wrestling crocodiles any day of the week. His lack of communication with his family would also have been far easier to explain to his gran. Instead he'd received a tongue-lashing over the phone from her that would've put even the fearsome Black Mamba in his place. Yet while he was in the doghouse with his gran, Connor received the good news that his mom's MS was in remission, for the time being at least.

Richie shut down his laptop and headed for the door. "Hey, it's pizza night in the cafeteria. Who's coming?"

Everyone started packing up, except Charley.

"I'll be along shortly," she said, then sighed. "Just finishing off the log."

"We'll save you a slice," yelled Ling, disappearing down the hallway with Jason.

As Marc hurried after them, Connor hung back. "I'll catch up," he said in answer to his friend's questioning glance.

Alone in the briefing room with Charley, Connor wondered how to broach the subject that had been on his mind since his return from Burundi. As he tried to pluck up the courage, Charley looked over and said, "You don't have to wait for me."

"No, it's okay," he replied, feeling even more nervous than he did before an assignment. "I've been wanting to ask you . . . do you want to go out sometime? Catch a movie or something together?"

Charley stopped typing. "Are you . . . actually asking me out on a *date*?"

She suddenly sounded as nervous as he was.

Connor nodded.

Charley's sky-blue eyes studied his face as if trying to judge whether he was joking. "Are you sure about this?"

"I've never been more sure," he replied, remembering his kiss with Amber and what had really been wrong about it. The simple fact was that it hadn't been Charley.

She spun her wheelchair toward him. "Because if you're serious, you need to understand how I ended up in this chair and how that's changed me."

"I want to know," said Connor, sitting down next to her. "I want to know everything about you."

Taking a deep breath, Charley steeled herself to revisit her past. "Well . . . This is the first time that I've ever told anyone the full story . . ."

Turn the Page for a Sneak Peek at

BODYGUARD

Book 7 : Target

PROLOGUE

The hot Californian sun glinted off the SUV's hubcaps as it cruised along the quiet suburban street. The man behind the wheel spotted a schoolgirl skipping on the sidewalk, his attention caught by her ponytail of golden-blond hair flicking from side to side. Judging from the carefree bounce in her step, she was no more than ten years old.

With a quick glance in his rearview mirror, the driver slowed down. He was almost alongside the girl when a voice cried out, "Charlotte!"

She stopped and turned. Another girl, petite with almond-shaped eyes, emerged from the porch of a large house. Her pink backpack rode high on her shoulders as she ran across the sun-baked lawn.

"*Ni hao*, Kerry!" Charlotte called back.

Her friend smiled warmly, revealing a set of braces. "Hey, your Chinese is getting good."

"I've been practicing," said Charlotte as the SUV continued past, unnoticed.

"You want to learn some more?" Kerry asked.

"Yeah," Charlotte replied eagerly. "We could use it as a secret code at school."

Kerry moved closer and whispered, "A best-friend language." She held up her little finger. "Friends forever?"

Charlotte entwined her own little finger around Kerry's. "Friends forever."

Then, hand in hand, they set off down the road. At the junction the silver SUV with tinted windows pulled up in front of them, and the passenger door swung open.

"Excuse me, girls," said the driver with a forlorn look. "Can you help me? I'm a bit lost."

They both stared at the man, taking in his bald head, reddened cheeks and beginnings of a double chin. Intrigued by his accent, Charlotte asked, "Are you from England?"

The man nodded. "I'm on vacation. I'm supposed to meet my daughter at Disneyland, but I got off the highway at the wrong exit."

"You really are lost," said Kerry. "Disneyland's in Anaheim. You're in North Tustin."

The man sighed and shook his head at the map on the passenger seat. "American roads! They're almost as wide as they are long. Can you show me exactly where I am?"

"Sure," said Kerry, leaning in to look at the map.

The man's eyes lingered briefly on Charlotte. Then he turned his full attention to Kerry.

Charlotte noticed an illuminated screen on the dashboard. "Why not use your GPS?" she suggested.

The man responded with a tight smile. "Can't work it for the life of me. Rental car."

Charlotte's eyes narrowed. His explanation was unconvincing; even her dad could work a GPS. "Kerry, I think we should be go—"

Before Kerry could move, the man rammed a stun gun against her neck. Kerry shrieked, her body juddering with a million volts. Her eyes rolled back and she fell limp. The man seized Kerry's backpack straps and, with a vicious tug, wrenched her body into the interior of the car.

Shocked by the speed of the attack, Charlotte stood rooted to the spot. She didn't try to grab Kerry, or even call for help. She just watched as the door slammed shut on her best friend. Then the SUV shot off, sped around a corner and disappeared.

The BODYGUARD Missions

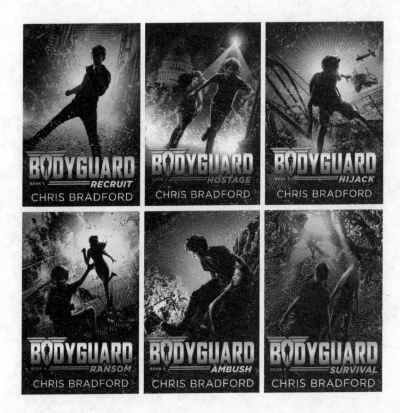

ACKNOWLEDGMENTS

Surviving as an author can be tough, but the challenges are much easier to overcome when you have a strong team around you:

Brian Geffen, editorial survival expert at Philomel Books—thanks for making the process as smooth and efficient as ever. Your constant supply of advice and encouragement has kept me going.

Michael Green, Publisher, an experienced hand at surviving the pitfalls of publishing. I truly appreciate your commitment and enthusiasm for the Bodyguard series.

Laurel Robinson, my copy editor, thanks for ensuring the manuscript stays on track for the States.

The whole team at Philomel for planning such a phenomenal launch to the series.

Most important of all, my valiant readers who have survived three missions with Connor! Keep up the good work and I hope you'll join us for the next stage of Bodyguard's journey . . .

Read, enjoy and stay safe!
Chris

Any fans can keep in touch with me and the progress of the Bodyguard series on my Facebook page or via the website at www.bodyguard-books.com.

Chris Bradford (www.chrisbradford.co.uk) is a true believer in "practicing what you preach." For his BODYGUARD series, Chris embarked on an intensive close-protection course to become a qualified professional bodyguard. His bestselling books, including the Young Samurai series, are published in more than twenty languages and have garnered more than thirty children's book award nominations internationally. He is a dedicated supporter of teachers and librarians in their quest to improve literacy skills and provides free teachers' guides to his books on his website. He lives in England with his wife and two sons.

Follow Chris on Twitter @youngsamurai.